D0232685

No Clock in the Forest

No Clock
in the
Forest

An Alpine Tale

Paul J. Willis

CROSSWAY BOOKS•WHEATON, ILLINOIS
A DIVISION OF GOOD NEWS PUBLISHERS

No Clock in the Forest: An Alpine Tale

Copyright © 1991 by Paul J. Willis

Published by Crossway Books, a division of
Good News Publishers, Wheaton, Illinois 60187.

All rights reserved. No part of this publication may be reproduced,
stored in a retrieval system or transmitted in any form by any means,
electronic, mechanical, photocopy, recording, or otherwise, without
the prior permission of the publisher, except as provided by USA
copyright law.

Cover design and illustration: Britt Taylor Collins

Map illustration: Laurie Vette

First printing, 1991

Printed in the United States of America

Library of Congress Cataloging-in-Publication Data
Willis, Paul J., 1955-
    No clock in the forest : an Alpine tale / Paul J. Willis.
       p. cm.
    I. Title.
PS3573.I456555N6 1991   813'.54—dc20   90-46781
ISBN 0-89107-599-2

99	98	97	96	95	94	93	92	91
15	14	13	12	11	10	9 8	7 6	5 4 3 2 1

For Sharon,
whose cares drop off
like autumn leaves

Rosalind: I pray you, what is't o'clock?

Orlando: You should ask me, what time o'day.
There's no clock in the forest.

Shakespeare,
As You Like It

Amoenas

North Queen

Center Queen

Chambers Lake

Obsidian

Demaris Cabin

Creek

Demaris

Tira

Three Queens Wilderness

L. VETTE

River
South Queen
William's Cave
Trail
The Bog
Lost Creek Meadows
Lost Creek Trail
Creek
Lost
Creek
Amoenas Gorge

1

As Garth drove through the last of the clear cuts, William leaned his head against the window of the car. He felt his skull rattle faintly and saw his own eyes in the outside mirror, moveably framed by fields of stumps all silvered and shattered and shifting by in a roadside dance of death. When he sat up straight, he saw a fat white chin, plopped in the glass like a scoop and a half of vanilla ice cream. He tensed his jaw and jutted it slightly. The effect was heroic; the effort, however, was hard to sustain.

Beyond William's reflection, the road passed into the forest and left the stumps behind. The amber signs that marked each curve began to hide in the reach of red cedar. At every turn the highway vanished, swallowed up in the greenest of worlds, an asphalt snake consumed by the garden. Garth slowed down as if to relish such a thought.

"Have you seen," he asked, "how the sword fern come to the road right here?" He held the wheel as a single frond, pendant with morning dew. He held it gently, so the dew would glisten where it was and not drip into his lap.

William turned and grunted. He saw the long white beard, thick like the lichen on the trees passing by. *Why*, he wondered, *had he ever agreed to climb a mountain with Garth?*

Climbing mountains was nothing new to William. Far

from it. By the count that he kept on the green-glow screen of his home computer, he had conquered sixty-six of them. He thought of himself as fairly accomplished, decently skilled, a real mountaineer. In short, the standard routes were beneath him now. What mattered were Serious Climbs. A Serious Climb held objective danger. It required boldness and commitment. It took fury in the heart and courage in a rucksack; it met the mountain on its very own terms. If William completed enough of these routes (or knocked them off, as he put it), he might one day be referred to as a Serious Climber. It would be whispered quietly behind his back at the Alpine Club. In years ahead he would flip through slides of his latest expeditions. The clubroom would be dark with awe. "Balstani tea is bloody wretched," he would say. "It's all we had for a week in the blizzard at Camp IV." Afterwards, total strangers would ask what kind of mittens he had worn on the summit day.

As of yet, he had not found time for the far-off ranges of the world on the weekends. So he sought his manhood in the local hills and found his partners at the Alpine Club meetings on Thursday nights. But on the last Thursday night, Garth had found *him*. The professor had marked him from across the room, edged to his side, taken his arm, and politely proposed they attempt the South Queen. For a moment, William was ecstatic. The northeast face was a climb he coveted. But the southwest slope was what Garth had in mind, which confirmed what everyone said of the man—that he only did walk-ups. This made Garth the worst sort of partner for an aspiring Serious Climber. So that should have been the end of it. William tried to edge away, but the old man held him with a glittering eye.

"Will you go?" said Garth.

"I will," said William. He answered with the surreal and sacred surprise of a bridegroom at a wedding ceremony.

So on this particular Saturday morning, Garth and William were trailhead bound, one watching ferns, the other regretting a weekend lost. William sighed, tuned in static on the radio, tuned it out, pushed up his sleeves, pushed them down, peeled his thumbnails, wished them back, and bent down to untie and retie his boots. That completed, he fished his ice ax from the seat behind him and held it on display. It was the mountaineer's tool, his rod and his staff, his terrible swift sword. And since the ax was newly purchased, it was more than worth discussing.

"New ax?" said Garth.

"New ax," said William. He drew a large breath before telling its secrets. "Seventy-centimeter. It's got a chrome-moly head, drooped pick, razor-cup adze, plus a laminated aluminum graphite and fiberglass shaft—so it won't vibrate. And the angle on the pick is adjustable." This he demonstrated, ratcheting the head of the ax in all directions. "The coating on the shaft is electrostatically applied—won't chip off like regular paint. Got it 35 percent off, too—at that warehouse place on Apple Street."

Garth checked the rearview mirror. "Old one break?"

"Uh . . . no," said William. "But this one handles lots better."

"Of course," said Garth.

William twisted around and put the ax away. He saw Garth's wooden ax on the back seat too. It was nearly as long as an antique alpenstock and battered enough to have been one. No ice tool, that—merely a cane for hobbling up snowfields. He kneeled backwards on the seat and ran his hand along the shaft. The wood was dark, smoky, smooth. In places he saw knots and whorls, obvious weak spots. One short fall on a boot-ax belay would snap it like a twig.

"How strong is yours?" he asked.

"As strong as you trust it will be," said Garth. For William it would not be strong.

He tried to guess the wood. Not laminated bamboo, certainly. Maybe ash, or hickory. He asked the old man.

"From the original," said Garth.

"Original what?"

"The original grove," Garth said. "The forest primeval."

William was not familiar with this kind. "But how well does the shaft take the shock on ice? Does it make your hand shiver?"

"Sometimes," said Garth, "it makes my hands tremble."

"I thought so," said William. He was pleased to have guessed the flaw.

He examined the head of the ice ax now, stroking the smooth and tarnished arc. He brushed the edge of the adze, the edge of the pick, both blunt with age. He stopped. Blunt were they? He drew back his fingertips, strangely numb. His own red blood was beading there. How could it? He brought his fingers to his lips and sucked them clean and held the taste in his mouth. The taste made him shiver. He checked beside him—Garth had not seen. Now his other hand traced the ax head, looking for the manufacturer's imprint. The metal was smooth. It bore no stamp.

"Where'd you buy this?" he asked.

"It was a gift," said Garth.

Maybe the shaft had a logo. William brushed his fingers down the wood once more. They stopped on a pattern of grooves so obvious that he blinked. Minutes ago the wood had been quite plain. He was sure of it. He doubled over the back of his seat to peer more closely. The car rounded a steep curve, and his head swarmed with motion sickness. But on the shaft, unmistakably, were hand-carved letters in an antique script. With a little scrutiny he traced three words: CAST ME AWAY. *Good idea,* he thought. He turned the shaft over. On the other side were three words more, carved in the same script: TAKE ME UP. That gave him pause. How could a person do both? He gripped the shaft tightly and trembled.

"Would you like to use it?" said Garth.

William dropped the ax as if it were the known instrument of a bizarre cult murder. He turned back around in the seat, his chin exhibiting new shades of pallor. "No," he said finally. "Thanks, but no. It's a little too long for serious ice." He had not meant to say *serious*—using the word for oneself was not done.

"It may be what you need," said Garth. "It's a serious ax." He left it at that.

So did William.

In a short while, Garth pulled into a shady turnout beneath a small waterfall. He switched off the key, and the motor shuddered three times—a repeated death rattle, or perhaps the violent exorcising of a stubborn demon. The car gave up its ghost—or stood quietly cleansed—and the two men stiffly got out. The air was cool on the small of their backs where their shirts had come untucked. Beside them, a neatly cut trail broke into the forest, not quite wide enough for two. A brown wood sign announced the itinerary:

Lost Creek Meadows   7
Obsidian Trail   8

Garth slipped away to the base of the fall and stood beneath a dogwood tree. Its blossoms were starting to wilt. The fading flowers trembled in a fine cool spray, and the spray fell softly on his beard. He paused to see the white foam splash, the black stones glisten. Then he knelt at the water's edge, and his knees sank deep in the mossy bank as he reached his lips to the stream. It was very good. He drank for the taste of melting snows and decaying cedars and settling must of fallen needles, for the fading damp and duff and detritus that made the water sweet. It was a taste far to be desired above the inside of an automobile, or for that matter, above the inside of the finest book. After his drink Garth stayed to consider the toil and spin of the waterfall, and lingered long.

Meanwhile William redeemed the time by donning his armor. Soon he towered beside the professor in full array: his feet were shod with white polyurethane; his shins were greaved with blue polypropylene; his loins were girded with beige polyester. His chest was mailed with a thoroughly waterproof, thoroughly breathable, thoroughly crimson parka. And his shoulders were hung with a marvelous burden, likewise crimson, looming behind him like a burning chest of drawers.

A concealed pocket behind his scalp held secret tools of navigation: a carefully folded contour map entitled "South Queen," laminated with clear contact paper to make it rainproof; *The Climber's Guide to the Three Queens,* second edition, in which every route he had mastered was duly checked and dated; a liquid-filled compass, magnifying glass attached; and a small altimeter. The altimeter was unreliable, but it did offer a number whenever it was consulted. William prized his digital watch for the same reason, even though it unaccountably stopped at times. Between his watch and his altimeter, no place and no moment lacked value.

Three accessory pockets festooned each side of the pack. One side held a plastic liter bottle that fizzed to capacity with miracle electrolytes; tropical chocolate bars, guaranteed not to melt; and a compact camera used only to record, and occasionally to contrive, the serious nature of William's exploits. The film in the camera had already been exposed six times to the downward plummet of an ice couloir, lost below in a foggy abyss.

In the other set of pockets lay a tube of Western Cwm

Cream ("as used by the conquerors of Mount Everest"); a mint-green stick of protective lip balm ("specially prepared to screen out dangerous high-altitude rays"); a small hand mirror to ensure proper application of both; a bottle of liquid amber soap ("Absolutely Biodegradable"); a plastic vial of insect repellent ("New! Improved! Stops Bugs Dead!"); a chartreuse toothbrush, part of the handle sawn off to save weight; a can of foot powder ("GETS THE ROT OUT!"); and a small cylinder of toilet paper (at home he carefully set aside each roll before it was completely used up).

This side of his pack was also home to exactly half of the Ten Essentials. Here lay a pair of prescription glacier goggles in a crush-proof lavender case; a lithium-cell headlamp—The Wonderbright; a waterproof box of waterproof matches; a silver whistle—The Acme Thunderer; and a red pocketknife, itself an arsenal. Folded into its recesses were tweezers, scissors, leather punch, awl, screwdrivers (flat blade and Phillips), cutting blades (short and long), toothpick, file, crosscut saw, can opener, bottle opener, corkscrew, and magnifying glass. The magnifying glass troubled William because he already had one on his compass. He often wondered whether he should vandalize his pocketknife to eliminate this redundancy.

And in the womb of William's pack? At the bottom, tightly curled like a slumbering fetus, a lime-green sleeping bag, quilted with down and laced with synthetic fibers. There too a canary-yellow air mattress. And beside it a bundle of fiberglass reeds, tightly wrapped in a purple shroud. Unleashed, they collected themselves like Ezekiel's bones to frame the nylon flesh of a geodesic dome.

Further inhabitants: a sackful of stove in bottles and tubes, a nesting set of aluminum pots, foil packets of freeze-dried delights, booties and gaiters and stockings and mittens, caps and cagoules and bandanas and . . . suffice it to say that these were a few of his favorite things.

Crushing it all was a 150-foot rattlesnake coil. No rope was needed for the snowfield they planned to climb, but William had packed it in the wan hope that Garth might be persuaded to try something More Interesting. Ice screws and pitons, nuts and carabiners, harness and helmet were stashed here too—just in case. William's versatile ice ax was strapped to attention on the back of his pack, its inverted head pillowed on a pair of black crampons. And that was all.

"Ready?" said William.

Garth left the waterfall and donned his own pack. It hung loosely on his shoulders, a weathered canvas bag of tricks. His coat was faded, a dubious gray. His pants were tattered khaki.

"Ready," said Garth. He waved his ax as if to say, "After you."

For the load that he carried, William took off with amazing strides. And his tongue kept pace with his feet. This was the maiden voyage of a new hip-belt suspension system—an ingenious concoction of snaps and buckles and Velcro straps—and William extolled its features for at least a full mile. As he talked, his palms cut diagrams in air, and he stared at them as if they would vanish if once he looked away. But since his student walked behind him, walled off from the blackboard, it did not really matter if the drawings were erased.

Garth was looking elsewhere anyway. His eyes kept track of the wandering stream beside the trail—purling in roots of red cedar, fanning over smooth logs, stopping in dark pools. In one dark pool—there!—flashed the orange belly of a newt.

Where the forest was thick, sword fern overhung the water. Where the forest was thin, the bracken foamed waist-high. Here they walked by faith, by a miraculous parting of pale green seas, and faith crushed the fiddleheads underfoot like so many sunken chariots. Shafts of sunlight, roiling with pollen, shed blessings on the ferny deep. The sunlight pierced an understory of vine maple, first to catch autumn fire. Slide alder grew in shadowy thickets, good reason for a trail. And dogwoods—one here, one there—dropped yellowing blossoms on the path.

Over the maple, the alder, the dogwood, sometimes shutting them off in darkness, great hemlocks and great cedars rose, giants on the earth. The cedar trunks were red and shaggy. Cobwebs hung in fire-scarred hollows, safety nets for cones and dust and dead leaf sprays. The hemlock trunks were gray and even, bearded with pale lichen. The huge trees groaned aloud at times, travailing in the heavy staccato of worlds torn apart—not any one tree, but all.

Yet the topmost branches held echoes of wind—soft, distant, the muted empyrean roar of a sea shell. From this verge of heaven, nudged by the breeze, hemlock cones leapt down to earth, littering the path, so small an incarnation of so great a tree. The cones fell almost soundlessly, touching the ground like shy-blown kisses. They slipped through William's diagrams as if through airy nothing.

William quit his lecture at last when the path upended itself in switchbacks over a valley step. Here he found comfort in merely breathing. He let his diagrams dissolve and fell to watching the manly rhythm of his polyurethane boots. Sometimes in midstride they clicked together like a gumball machine.

And so miles passed, hours passed. The two men watered the path with the sweat of their brows, anointing change in the green world about them. Cedars and hemlocks slipped away. Douglas fir appeared, then vanished. True firs raised their straight-brushed steeples, sticky with cones that squirrels sever. Cones like gently curved bananas hung from tall white pine. Then mountain hemlocks, shorter than their lowland cousins, drooped their limp crowns, each one crooked like the hat of a witch. Last of all grew whitebark pine, wind-raked clumps of rubbery twigs, refuge in a storm.

Ferns gave way to mops of bear grass. Mossy earth dried up in dust. Then came a snow patch, hollow and arched like the shell of a tortoise. The surface was scalloped, stained with needles. William broke through into meltwater pools, and Garth followed after, wetting his cracked leather boots. It was then that his nose caught the first sweet sting of alpine slopes. Here was manna at their feet, hinting a promised land.

And before very long it was upon them. The forest simply ended, and they stood on the verge of a vast meadow park-land. Except for islands of hemlock and whitebark, all was treeless, open to the bright sky. The land lay green, lavish and undulating, dotted with ponds and ahum with mosquitoes. All of this, paradise enough, was but a velvet footstool to the raised splendor of the South Queen. They lifted their eyes to its snowy fullness.

"Ah," sighed Garth. His burden slipped unbidden from his shoulders.

"Ah!" cried William. "Aiee!" He slapped his temple and reached one hand behind him to his pack. There, his wrist painfully bent, he unzipped the waiting pocket and seized upon the magic vial within. He had what he wanted. It pooled yellow in his palms. The bitter poison stung his eyes and crept between his lips.

2

A COLD FOG CAME upon the meadows that night, and dawn did not turn it away. By midmorning the fog still hung white and thick, bending down the meadow grasses under wet frost. Somewhere in the blank swirl, a pika squeaked. Elsewhere, a marmot whistled. And from the cluttered depths of William's pack came the delighted squeals of a pair of chipmunks, feasting on tropical chocolate bars that will not melt. Periodically the chipmunks issued out from the pack to parade their success around the camp with toilet-paper confetti.

Such joy was only possible because the master was away. For at this moment, high on the mountain, William was trudging in wet, soft snow, stepping where Garth had stepped. The mountainside was foggy too. The snow gave the fog an opaque radiance, and the tinted goggles that William wore did little to help him see. Garth, however, was noticing things. He had first pointed out an invisible pair of rosy finches. Then he had bid William kneel before a spider in a suncup. Now Garth stopped so abruptly that William bumped into him.

"Have you seen," he said, "how the algae bloom?" He pointed to the pink sides of a suncup, blood-red at the bottom. "Watermelon snow, it's called. Even tastes like watermelon. Try some."

He scooped and offered a mittenful. William took it with

the strange reluctance of a grown man accepting a candy cane from a department store Santa Claus.

"Not too nourishing for us, but the ice worms thrive on it. Tiny ones, no bigger than the hairs on your chest."

William looked down and mentally X-rayed his red parka. He had always been aware of the lack of any real hair on his chest. He rarely took his shirt off.

"You seldom see them," said Garth. "In fact, I've only seen them once in my life. It was a very sunny day, late afternoon on the Center Queen. Suddenly, where minutes before there had been only snow, the glacier was wriggling with thousands of ice worms, bursting forth like upstart flies from the mud of the Nile. Spontaneous generation."

Before Garth finished speaking, a group of ravens swirled from the fog. They brayed in William's ear and vanished, still clamoring, a cloud of witnesses. One returned and, passing closer, chuckled aloud. William had never heard a raven chuckle. What was the joke? What did ice worms have to do with the mud of the Nile?

They switched the lead. William plodded up into the fog, not at all sure where snow and sky met, for each shone white, dazzling, effulgent. The harder William strained his eyes, the more he merely saw the tiny flashes, the hallucinogenic explosions, that his eyes created to fill the void. Mentally he marked a spot for each foot to rest, but the foot would find purchase while still in midair—a miracle of levitation. He walked as if on a dark stairway. But it was not dark—his feet were groping in glorious light.

Garth, fortunately, had climbed the route before and was sure of the way. Occasionally he tapped William on the shoulder and pointed his ice ax through the fog. At these moments they exchanged the ritual hope that the summit would break above the clouds, but William told himself he did not really care. A real mountaineer, a Serious Climber, did not come for the view. The important thing was to complete the climb, and to do so with daring efficiency.

It was nearly midday when a breeze met their faces. The summit was nigh. Ragged red rocks thrust out of the snow like half-sown dragon teeth, shredding the fog. The snowfield channeled in all directions, but the way was clear—earlier climbers had left a dirty trough. This they followed through the rocks to a cinder path at snow's end. The cinder path, in a very few steps, led them at last to a cast-iron box. It lay at their feet between two basalt horns like a toppled tombstone. William and Garth each grabbed the side of a horn and leaned over the brink of the northeast face into the wind. They saw nothing.

"We're here," said Garth.

William did not reply. He kneeled by the iron box and twirled the wing nuts that clamped it shut. They squeaked in the wind, as did the hinges when he opened the lid. He reached inside and plucked a battered ledger from a nest of four pencil stubs, two dried pens, one flattened tube of zinc oxide, innumerable moleskin scraps, a calling card for Inevitable Life Insurance, and choice droppings of an alpine rodent.

Still kneeling on the cinders, William opened the ledger. The last entry was two days old:

> *"Praise the Lord Jesus! He helped me every step of the way! Thank you God for your fantastic creation! He's my Redeemer—he saved my soul! Christ is King!"*

The preceding passage bore the most foul language imaginable, and climaxed with a rhetorical question.

> *"It's cold up here! How do I get down?!"*

On the opposite page, a group from You-Can-Do-It Expeditions had left their mark:

> *"My first climb!! I can't believe I did the whole thing!!"*
> *"Sweet. But don't look down."*
> *"This is my second time. A real breeze (ha-ha)."*
> *"I love you, Scotty, wherever you are!"*
> *"I never thought I'd make it, but Walter wouldn't let me quit, so I really didn't have much choice, did I?"*
> *"I'm going to come back and bring Harvey, my dog."*
> *"Hey, I climbed the little sucker!"*
> *"I would like to dedicate this climb to Linda, who had to stay in camp today because she was throwing up. She's been such an inspiration to us all."*

William turned back a few pages, forcing them against the wind.

> *"NE face—<u>definitely</u> grade IV. The bergschrund is a bitch this time of year. Heavy stonefall in the hourglass. <u>Very</u> hard ice. 12 hrs. from Lira Col."*

William took note. He had a special place in his home computer for these tidbits. Then a nearby entry in delicate script caught his eye:

> *"So fully cosmic to partake of the oneness of earth and this universe, united at this lonely apex by our individual souls encompassing the goodness of all terrestrial forces indivisible with sun and moon, triumphant in our eternal bonds, freed by the all-loving sasquatch mother of mankind and every creature gathered in eternal celebration of the energy of our togetherness and aloneness, ebbing and flowing in one wind, one tide, one womb of the universal cosmos."*

William turned back to the most recent entry and selected

a pencil stub from the box. He did not care for effusion, but he did enjoy a public record of his achievements. "William Arthur, #67," he wrote. His signature surprised him—a childish leaden scrawl. He was colder than he knew.

An involuntary shiver stood him up, and he gave the ledger and pencil stub to Garth. "Here," he said, and pretended to stare off the northeast face while looking out of the corner of his eye to see what Garth would write. "Garth Foster," he saw. And then, "Get their glad tidings." Glad tidings? What tidings? Whose tidings? Where gotten? People must say what they mean. It was one thing to be unclear by accident, but another—an unforgivable thing—to be so by intent.

Meanwhile, the breeze poured through his very bladder and seized it with a chill. He descended several steps farther than he needed to and turned his back on Garth and the wind. There he assumed the time-honored stance, and there he found relief. And there, *in media res*, a shift in the wind left relief unconsummated.

No little shift. A gust of cinders raked his teeth and filled his ears. He staggered back. His parka billowed out like a sail. He spun around, and the crimson sail reversed itself to swelling pregnancy. His cap! It flew into the fog before him. He reached for it much too late, and his reach gave the wind the advantage it needed. It pounced and knocked him to his knees, bellowing triumph. Such wind as this, so fierce, so sudden, he could not remember.

He crouched in the cinders and shut his eyes, groveling before the summit as if in abject worship. What of Garth? He peeked upwards. All he could see was boiling fog. He had once read of a man that was literally blown from a mountaintop in a freak storm. Maybe Garth could hang on to one of the horns.

The wind blasted a rift in the fog, and William looked.

The old man was still there, his coat snapping like a flag. He was not crouching on the ground like William. He was not clutching at the lava horns. He was, to William's astonishment, standing fully upright between the two rocks, straddling the iron box with his feet. He was chesting the storm, welcoming it with arms outstretched as if it blew some preternatural energy into his heart. The antique ax sailed high in his hand. The wind tore at the old man's beard, parting it like an angry sea, and his long white hair was streaming behind him. Garth was speaking, but not to William. Great guttural chords and rumbling diphthongs rolled into the storm, louder than the wind itself. The words, if that is what they were, sounded long and deep, old and strong. They rode upon the wind, and spurred it, called it into being.

William listened, prostrate in the cinders. The wind searched him to an aching core, and he clenched and shivered with bony cold, remembering the time that a boulder the size of a millstone had flown past his ear on a silent mountainside. That had been just as real, and unreal.

Garth stood unmoved, speaking into the tempest, speaking more urgently now. The wind, if anything, blew more strongly. It whipped his coat about him like an old and tattered robe. William sensed that something was about to happen, and his voice welled up unbidden within him. "No!" he shouted. Without knowing why, he chanted it out: "No! No! No!" The words were high-pitched, puny, the wail of a child. Garth gave no sign of hearing them. The ice ax swung across the clouds, and as it swung, the words and the wind more deeply roared. All at once the fog rushed into the swirling robe. And Garth was gone. For an instant, William saw the ice ax gleaming overhead—alone, disembodied, the thing itself. Then it too disappeared, cast away in the fog.

That changed everything.

Immediately the wind expired, the mists hung still, all

was bright calm. William slowly raised himself, groping for the violence gone from the air. He looked about fearfully, braced for a blast from any quarter. But none came. He walked unsteadily, like an infant, the few short steps to the summit. There, on the lid of the iron box, a single snowflake softly melted.

3

"NO TOILET PAPER? NONE?" Grace was appalled.

The youngest boys were snickering at her. She brutalized them with a glance, and then checked the other faces in the circle. The older one with the curly hair—what was his name? Lance. Lance sat perfectly cross-legged, aloof and inscrutable. Grace could not tell what he thought about twelve days without toilet paper, which was too bad. It would be nice to have Lance on her side. The girl in braids beside him looked absolutely serene—as if she never ate anything but yogurt and lentil soup, and freedom from toilet paper would be one more step to complete holiness. The two girls sitting next to her, however, seemed less destined for ascetic purity. Their faces were blanched with shock. But they were weak. They would go along with using sticks and rocks.

"Snow works best actually," said the leader. He was a young man with glasses and a woolly red beard.

"What about lava!" screamed the smallest boy. "That would clean you out!" He convulsed with giggles and tipped over backwards in the dirt. Grace noticed that Lance was ignoring him, and again she hoped for an ally. She caught his glance and rolled her eyes toward the little screamer. But Lance looked away, ignoring her too.

A nutcracker screeched in the whitebark pine overhead. "Too bad for you!" it seemed to say. "Too bad for you!" Grace stared up into its hard black eye. She made it relent. The bird flew away across the meadows, diminished itself to a dark silhouette against the cloud-wrapped mountain.

"Bury it at least six inches deep," said the leader. "You should be able to stand on the dirt barefoot when the hole is filled up."

"Eeeooohh!" said the two girls next to Grace. They looked down at their new waffle-stompers in disgust, imagining their bare toes mired in their own fresh offal. There were more snickers from across the circle.

"Make sure you're at least a hundred feet away from any lake or stream. And we don't wash our pots in the lakes and streams either."

We? thought Grace.

She slapped a mosquito on her calf, and the sucked blood burst across her carefully shaven skin. She tried to wipe it off, but the blood and mosquito fragments mixed with the dust and damp already there. Mile upon mile they had hiked that day in filth and in fog. When the fog had lifted, the mosquitoes had descended. Her thighs were swollen white with welts, some of them dug into bloody craters by the tips of her well-filed fingernails. All day they had hiked, bearing hideous burdens. Her shoulders ached from the abuse. And the leader had lied. He had lied about how far it was. At their last rest in the woods he had said there was only a half-mile left. That was hours ago. They had just arrived at this patch of dirt which he called camp.

The mountains did not seem to be Grace's sort of place. She was more of a valley girl, she thought. And now she knew just what she thought: What utter bliss to be back at the trailhead, hopping into a low white sports car. She would not even put her pack in the trunk. Thump! It fell from her shoulders and hit the dust, sprawled on its back like a helpless potato bug. Slam! The door shut her into a vinyl chamber, spotlessly red, pulsing like a sinewy heart at the urge of a stereo tape deck. The car leapt to the road as with muscled thighs. She rolled down the window and the air poured by, winnowing hapless mosquitoes from her hair. Beside her, raking through the gears around hairpin turns, the wheel firm in his grasp, was Lance.

Lance? Grace blushed. She looked at him as if he could have heard. But there was no danger. Lance was listening intently to the leader.

"Right," said the leader, "if you want to know how far we've come, look at your map. A couple of you ought to have one. Grace, don't you?"

"I dunno," she said. It was an affront to expect her to keep track of such a thing.

"You ought to know," the leader said firmly. "Each of you should know what you're carrying."

"I have a map," said the girl with braids. She held it out to the leader.

"No, Jennifer, it's for you to look at. Try and figure out how far we've hiked."

With Lance's help, she carefully unfolded the map and laid it out on a poncho in the middle of the circle. A slight breeze overturned it; one of the younger boys grabbed some rocks and plunked them on the edges. The rocks shed grit that rattled on the map.

"All right, how many miles to the inch?" said the boy.

"You mean inches to the mile, stupid." That was his friend.

"One inch to a mile," said Lance. "It says down here."

"Who's got a ruler?" asked one of the more frightened girls.

"No, first we have to find out where we are," said the other.

"We're right here under this tree!" yelled the smallest boy.

He giggled uncontrollably. "Don't you know that, stupid?" It felt marvelous to so deftly assess a total stranger.

The girl felt quite small, however, even though she knew the boy was what her mother would call immature.

"Maybe get where you can see the map, Grace." This was the leader's suggestion.

She was not about to. That leader thought he was the grand wonderful master of ceremonies.

"Did we start here?" asked Lance. He pointed to a spot in a sea of green where a black dotted line met a red-and-white-striped one.

"What do the rest of you think?" asked the leader.

Everyone shrugged his shoulders, except Grace, who was searching for a mosquito on her forehead. She slapped it dead, and then looked the leader bang in the eye.

"Who cares?" she said.

"You'll care," he told her, "when you're lost in the wild."

The mosquitoes went away when the cool darkness came. Grace put her head outside her sleeping bag. At last there was no tiny whining in her ears, no hot-itch needles probing her cheeks. But now she shivered, almost epileptically. She had been advised to wear a wool cap, but she was not wearing one. A wool cap might give her split ends. At the very least, it would mat down her hair.

She lay on the verge of a plastic tarp next to the boy who giggled. Regrettably, Lance was sleeping several bodies away. She would have arranged the bags differently, but she had been sent to the creek to wash the supper pot and had come back to find everything laid out. It would have been too bold a move to rearrange the bags. Further, she had been told that the pot was not clean enough—there was still some bulgur burned on the bottom. She did not like the stuff (vulgar, she called it—how Lance had downed three bowls of it she never would know); she enjoyed scouring the burnt kernels even less. Grace had stomped away and, in a courageous gesture of civil disobedience, washed the pot right in the creek. But rebellion has its price—the creek water had numbed her hands beyond belief.

As far as she could tell, everyone was asleep but herself. Twice the little giggler had kneed her in the back as he jerked in his slumbers. Both times she repaid him with a kick to the shins, but he did not awaken, and she envied him. Grace felt she might more easily fall asleep on a concrete floor. She had tried every position and found them all wanting. What's more, her new down jacket made an utterly inferior pillow. Bunched one way, it formed a lump no softer than Jacob's stone. Stretched out more evenly, it slumped her head so that she lay with her jaw tilted up like a model candidate for artificial respiration. When the down was plumped to the right loft, a zipper or snap invariably stuck in her ear.

At home, Grace's parents had just bought her a waterbed, and she had soon become used to it, the way she became used to all the things they gave her. This mountain trip was also their gift. She had begged to go after seeing the slide show at her high school for You-Can-Do-It Expeditions. She saw golden boys and dark slim girls, arm in arm amid deep purple wildflowers. They went splashing together in the sandy shallows of a hundred sparkling lakes. They sent up silver sprays of snow as they slid down crystal slopes. They cuddled close around night's glowing embers. It was more than midsummer's dream come true. After her mother had carefully inquired over the phone about the safety record of You-Can-Do-It Expeditions, Grace was given the money to go.

Just this morning her parents had brought her to the dusty base camp. They stayed long enough to meet her leader, then glided away. When the chrome-spoked wheels had disappeared, the young man with the red beard—so nice at first—began to chide her for not having broken in her boots. Then he rifled through her suitcase and confiscated her nail polish, shampoo, and portable stereo headphones. Before she could object, another car crawled tentatively into sight, anxious parents frozen in the front seat, terror-stricken child in the back. The leader turned with an open smile.

From over the mountain the gibbous moon emerged full in her face. Now she surely would not sleep. She half sat up and watched the silvered bodies beside her, their knees drawn up in fetal slumber. Only Lance lay flat on his back. She thought she could hear the rhythm of his breathing, but lost track of it when the boy beside her abruptly flipped and began to snore, an asthmatic soprano. As a mere matter of routine justice, Grace readied a vicious kick. But she paused. Her eyes swept over the brightly lit meadow to the dark forest verge, and there came to her a wonderful notion, poking into the moonlit night like a fiddlehead in the forest.

She would leave.

The audacity of it suited her perfectly. She would flee in the moonlight, escape in the dark, run away in the night—all of those things. Yes! she told herself. The plan trembled and grew and luxuriated in the nourishing rays of the moon. She would walk to the trailhead—downhill every step—and in the morning hitchhike home. She could tell her parents she had gotten sick, and that the leader had put her on a bus, and that she had had to walk home from the terminal because she couldn't get through on the phone, or because she didn't have any money for the call, or—or—no matter, she could fix that later. But now—now was the appointed time to leave.

Should she wake up Lance? Her gaze rested on his upturned face, curls shining, lips slightly parted. But close beside him, almost touching his ear in the moonlight, was the braided brow of the girl called Jennifer. Grace knew. She would leave alone.

Now she had reason to stay awake, and oddly enough, she yawned. The air began to chill her shoulders. She thought how warmly they might nest back again in her bag. A moment's rest before she set out, the briefest nap—that was all she asked. She would not leave now, but then. She sank back. Her eyelids closed.

Had not some small creature chosen just this moment to traverse the length of her sleeping bag, this story would be much shorter than it is. As it was, Grace sat fully upright and awake and slid on her down jacket. And in one stroke having destroyed her pillow, she had no choice but to go through with it. Quietly, she swung her legs out from the bag and hitched up her shorts. Her thighs exploded in myriad goose bumps. A clothing list had required wool pants, but it had not been a requirement to her taste. *Keep moving,* she told herself. *On with the boots. You can do it.* Her fingers stumbled over the laces. Then carefully she stuffed her bag in a tight nylon sack—most of it, anyway. She rolled up her pad in a spongy scroll. In the moonlight it was easy to strap the pad and the bag to the bottom of her pack.

Silently she withdrew from her pack a few issued items: a silver bottle of white gasoline, a bulging sack of freeze-dried carrots, a gleaming helmet, a limp harness, and some sort of ice pick—she hadn't been told what it was. What about the map? She held it in her hand. No, it didn't weigh much. Yes, it might be useful. But she knew the path. And she couldn't read it anyway. The map joined the other discards on the ground.

She set her pack against the tree, sat down, wiggled into the straps. Even with the lightened load, she stumbled on arising and lurched back to correct herself. A small branch snapped. The report rang soft as thunder. On cue, the red-bearded leader sat up like Lazarus called from the tomb. Grace froze in the shadow of the tree. The leader groped in a boot for his glasses. Then he groped in another boot—no glasses. He peered at the sleepers beside him. He peered at the branches above him. He peered at the trunk and its moon-shadow. Then he hung his head in his lap and meditatively picked his nose. In a few minutes he lay back down and began breathing heavily.

When the leader was most certainly asleep again, Grace slipped out of the shadow and away from the camp. She stepped softly in the grass, as if stalking a chipmunk, and at length she found the trail (not right away, because the leader had insisted they camp out of sight from all other wilderness travelers). Her boots shone wet from the dew in the meadow, but now they dulled in little puffs of silver smoke. The path sloped down to the forest edge, easy to follow. She could not get lost.

There is something exhilarating about walking alone and in secret by moonlight. Grace felt giddy and sure and strong, summoned to shout to the stars that shone for her alone and not for sleepers. Over her shoulder the mountain glowed huge and white. Before her the meadows unrolled pale splendor. The night was good and she was in it.

But she entered the forest all too soon. There the night was not so good. It was like walking into a dark cellar of a strange house, and groping for a light cord that someone has told you is "right there," and not finding it, and brushing against soft dusty sofas, and stepping on piles of boards that rattle, and wondering if some of the boards have nails, and suddenly finding cobwebs that stick on your face in fragments, and wondering if a spider might have gotten onto your face too. There weren't so many cobwebs in the forest, but there was no hope of a light cord either. The moon did not penetrate the darkness of the canopy, and Grace had neither candle nor flashlight.

She had not walked far when her knees and toes collided with something firm but soft. A little scream escaped her, an exaggerated hiccup. Her legs rubbed up against pulsing fur: a bear. She knew. It must be asleep. It must have fallen asleep on the trail. She had not awakened it. Or maybe she had. Maybe it was just pretending to be asleep. She stood very still for a long time.

Then, slowly, she inched backwards, taking very short steps. Suddenly her calves touched more soft fur. Despair thrilled her. It was another bear, this one also feigning sleep. They had trapped her. Once again she stood very still. Then she moved her foot sideways. No good—there it touched the bear's paw outstretched on the ground. She moved her other foot—it met the other paw. She was standing in its arms!

Grace shivered miserably. Maybe—and this was her only hope—maybe she could step over the paw and run away. She lifted her foot and extended it far to the side—slowly, softly, the way she had learned in ballet. *Farther*, she thought. *Farther*. But one extra inch cost Grace her balance. Backwards she tumbled into the waiting jaws of death. But death only put a splinter in her thumb. The two bears, clever to the last, had transformed themselves into mossy stumps.

She took a deep breath and picked herself up. Her feet shuffled over the soft duff till they found the path from which they had strayed. The trail was firm and good. She felt relieved, but only a little. She thought of the seven sleepers now, at peace in the bright meadows, and of her empty spot at the edge of the tarp. For a moment she paused. It was not too late. It was not too far. She could still . . . and she could yet . . . But for some reason—the inertia of pride, perhaps—she continued, barely picking each boot off the path for fear of losing the way again.

She heard things. First the stream came creeping by. The water bubbled darkly, swirling and sucking almost at her feet. It asked for her by name. Then it receded into silence. That was worse, for Grace then feared she was lost. The trail stayed on the bank of the creek the entire way, did it not? A little creature skipped over her tracks and froze her in them. She heard it scour the brush. Then groans and creaks shot overhead, squealing like doors on rusty hinges. These were only trees, she knew, but were the groans too loud, too full, for a windless night in the forest? Down the trail the stream swung near again; the rushing water covered all sounds else. This was not good. It is what you cannot hear that finds you.

And she ran into things. She tripped over roots. She hit her shins on boulders. Sharp dry limbs plucked the down from her jacket. Tendrils of maple reached into her hair. Once she missed a turn on the trail and planted her face in the trunk of a tree. The moon shone into little clearings, but here she waded through bracken fern that kept her steps in darkness. The wet fronds slithered across her thighs, sent rivers of dew to her ankles.

The night stumbled on, fraught with terrors, and at length Grace grew too tired to care. All the horrors of sleeping bears and darkling streams and grasping limbs and slithery things amounted to naught before an almighty yawn. She grew not only tired—she grew cross, and said a great many things to the red-bearded leader in her mind. "If I hit my shin just one more time," she threatened him, "I'll quit. I will." No sooner had the words been said than she caught her shin on the corner of a rock. She half-pronounced a fearful curse and sat down. She meant to keep her promise—at least until daylight.

Grace knew she was somewhere between four miles and four yards from the highway. That would have to do. She dragged out her sleeping bag, threw it on the trail, and crawled inside, head downhill. Her boots were still on, and her sleeping pad stayed strapped to her pack. A tangle of roots brought their knees to her spine, but Grace hardly noticed. Soon she was snoring as prettily as the boy she had left in the meadow.

The night was far gone. One short hour brought dawn's early light, and two hours more saw the sun shine into the low forest valley. But neither dawn nor sunrise awakened Grace. The light lay dappling over her eyelids, and she slept on.

What awakened her was a voice. "Who do you think you are?" it said.

4

GRACE OPENED HER EYES to see the voice. Overhead hung a twisted face, round and pale like the full moon. *The man in the moon,* she thought. His lips were pursed, his eyes hollow. Grace closed her eyes again. She would pretend to be asleep, like a tree stump.

It didn't work.

"You heard me," said the face. "Who are you?"

"Me?" said Grace. "I'm just a poor wayfaring stranger."

"Ah," said the man in the moon—as if he had learned something. "Do you always sleep on trails?"

"I do when I'm tired," she yawned. She sized him up and found him wanting. "Listen, how far is the trailhead from here?"

An arm appeared and waved in a circle. "This is it," said the face.

Languidly, Grace raised herself on one elbow and looked down the path. Not twenty steps away, it plunged into another field of bracken. Nearby, the stream cascaded down a mossy falls. Grace strained her eyes for the white sports car of her dreams, or at least for smooth pavement. She saw only ferns, waving in the sun, and beyond the ferns, thickets of alder.

"Where's the road?" she asked.

"I wish I knew," said the face, only now it was an entire

man in a torn red parka that rustled and squeaked like aluminum foil.

"So it's down the trail a ways?" she pressed.

"What trail is that?" said the man.

"Why, the trail we're on—what else?"

He wagged his head. "Sorry," he told her. "No more trail." By the way that he spoke, Grace knew that at least for her sake he was not sorry at all. "This," he announced, sweeping both arms, "is the end."

"But there's no road," Grace insisted.

"Precisely," said the man. "There is no road." He stood back with arms folded, pleased, it seemed, with the novel concept of a roadless trailhead.

Grace decided to drop it. She must have come down the wrong trail in the dark. She got out of her sleeping bag and made a show of poking around in her pack. She knew just what she wanted from the man.

"Could you spare a little breakfast?" she asked. "I seem to have eaten most of my food." She smiled her breezy smile.

Without answering, the man turned and walked to the clearing. Grace followed, dragging her pack and sleeping bag behind her. The man was right; the trail simply ended in the ferns. They waded into full sunshine and stopped next to a tall red pack. The ferns beside it were crushed into a bathtub of green. The man pulled a plastic bag from the pack and gave to her a chipmunk's portion of store-bought granola.

Suddenly he swore aloud. More granola was dribbling out of a freshly chewed hole in the plastic. "This needs to last," he explained.

"That all you have?" she asked.

"Pretty much. Unless—" His voice trailed off. His eye came to rest on a weathered canvas packsack strapped atop his own. Here was a place he seemed to have overlooked. He unstrapped the packsack, untied the drawstring, and thrust in his arm. He groped in every corner. There—he had something. He brought up the booty—a fist-sized globe wrapped in a piece of paper. He quickly shed the wrapping and held up an apple.

"Want a bite?" he asked. Before she could answer, he took one himself. His teeth sank deep. His eyes lit up with pain and surprise. He plucked the apple from his mouth and roared. "It broke my bloody tooth!" he cried and looked at the apple as if it had bitten him.

"What's this?" he said. His fingers dug through the juicy pulp and extracted a dripping key. He held it up and let the apple drop in the ferns (where Grace snatched it). They looked at the key together. It had two flat teeth, a cylindrical shaft, and an ornate ring on the end. There were a few spots of orange rust. Grace had seen no key like it. She wondered what it opened.

"Did it really break your tooth?" she asked.

The man checked with his thumb. "Maybe not," he said. "Feels like it should have." He laughed abruptly and shoved the key in his pocket. That was that, he seemed to say. No use troubling about it.

His eyes then fell on the crumpled paper in his hand. He smoothed it out and inspected both sides. Something snagged his interest. He held the paper up close to his face and moved his lips silently. "It's some kind of poem," he said aloud. His voice held a trace of disgust. He shoved the paper at Grace. "Here," he said. "You like poetry?"

She shrugged her shoulders. "A little," she mumbled. She wiped the granola crumbs from her palms and took the paper. She would humor the man for a few more minutes, and then leave. Her mistake, however, was to glance at the script.

All at once her lips faltered, her fingers trembled. She knew whose writing it was—knew it better almost than her own. The carefully etched hand echoed in her memory from a myriad of birthday letters and lengthy notes composed upon "special occasions"—The Hoary Marmot Holiday, The Trillium Tragoo, The Feast of Free Waters. (There were many others, and even in her youngest years she had half an idea they were improvised for her sake.) All of the letters, once cherished, now discarded, concluded in the same way: "Your affectionate uncle . . ."

The paper grew hot and slippery in her hands. She was afraid the stranger would change his mind and take it back, and that made the poem quite hard to read:

> *A gentle wight for gentle ladies three*
> *Aduentured through a verdant wood newgrowne,*
> *Through wildernesse that mote a wastlond bee,*
> *Vnless he greete the greenwood for his owne,*
> *Vnless he know the leaf as ice and stone.*
> *Faine needs he find a maid of faerie eyne,*
> *To spie the shielde vpon the second throne,*
> *To limn therein the ledgers ancient line—*
> *Lest Beast and woman darke the northerne morning*
>   *shyne.*

Grace read the stanza three times over, swiftly moving her lips. It was just like him: beasts and thrones and fairies—the sort of thing he always had written her. She tried to feel scornful. It didn't work.

The man began to eye her suspiciously. He looked as if he wondered why he had been so generous with the paper. "What does it say?" he demanded, and snatched it away. He read the poem again, brows knit. "What nonsense," he announced, and stuffed the paper into a little compartment at the top of his pack.

Grace folded her arms fiercely. Who likes to have things torn from their hands? She was angry—and curious. "That your pack?" she asked, pointing to the canvas heap in the ferns.

"My friend's," said the man. He did not sound very convincing.

"So where's your friend?"

"My friend? He—ah—went down the other side of the mountain. I was going to meet him."

She gave a dissatisfied nod. What would her uncle be doing up here with such a fool as this? She, for one, could do without him. She stepped to the waterfall and drank deeply, then returned. Her plans were made: another getaway.

"Thank you for breakfast," she said politely. "Very kind of you."

The man was recoiling the intestines of his pack. He didn't answer. Perhaps he, in turn, could do without her.

"I really must go now," said Grace. "This isn't the trail I wanted at all."

The man still took no notice. He couldn't get his air mattress to fit.

There was room in Grace's pack for her sleeping bag, so she threw it inside instead of strapping it on the bottom. "Goodbye," she said sorting her arms through the shoulder straps. Her voice quavered a little.

He barely looked up. "See you," he grumbled, and waved her off. The man returned to the bowels of his pack, and Grace strode into the trees.

She was reasonably sure she had missed a trail junction in the dark. The trail they had taken the day before began at a road, not a patch of ferns. And it followed a creek the entire way. Had she followed that same creek all night long? She must have changed creeks somewhere. But then she would be on the left bank instead of the right bank, for she had crossed no bridges. Yet that would only be true going downstream. Going upstream, the near bank of the old creek would match the right bank of the new creek. And the bank closest to her now was on the right. Although, if she were standing in the water it would be on the left, which would make it the left bank. Facing downstream, however, it would still be the right bank, which proved—what? She had forgotten. She had taken the wrong path. She would leave it at that. Meanwhile, best to watch out for the red-bearded leader in case he came looking for her.

Her head felt light from little sleep. But as she walked, her limbs awoke to the morning. The forest was a green and gentle place by day. The stream, so evil-sounding in the dark, now purled at her feet. One bird chanted a single note that calmly echoed through the trees. A chipmunk raced beneath her feet and down the path, tail erect. Grace laughed at him. "Why run?" she called. "I won't hurt you." The chipmunk eyed her for just a moment, and then dashed into a green-shine patch of thick salal.

She stooped to see where it had gone and saw a bed of twinflowers. Each pair of blossoms hung shyly downcast, a lavender inch from the ground. She touched one softly. And there were more flowers. She saw white pointed petals of delicate queen's cup, six to the lily. She saw tiny coolwort, dappling the ground like forest sunlight. She saw pink-striped candy flowers, cupping the dew. On she sauntered, her eyes alerted. There in the shadows, the red pulp explosion of coral-root. And there in the ferns, the tight orange ball of a tiger lily. Here, thigh-high, the chalk-green stalks of pearly everlasting. And here, head-high, the thrust of corn lily, crowned with clusters of green and white blossoms. Grace did not know any names for these flowers, but they looked as lovely and smelled as sweet, without them even so.

She took thought, as she walked, of her uncle's poem. It was curious—a poem like that in a place like this. Could she recite it? She tried, stumbled, stopped. This brought panic.

She resolved to write down what she could. You-Can-Do-It Expeditions had required her to bring pen and notebook. She still had them, she hoped. Forty feet above the path she spied a cedar of gigantic girth. She clambered to it and parked her pack on the backside of the trunk, out of sight from the trail. The pen and paper were there in her pack, sticky beneath the mangled apple. She sat down to record.

First she repeated the lines to herself, stroking her hair when memory failed. Then she rushed to put down each word before it left her mind. Before long, she was fairly sure she had it. She understood the poem no better after writing it out. But it felt more familiar. Her own fingers had stroked the words into being—they were partly hers now. And insofar as the words belonged to her uncle, they were the closest friends she had.

Not so very long ago, Grace and Garth had been quite inseparable. He an old bachelor, she his only niece—that explained it for most people. Grace recalled his knotty hand that led her up the dark stairs to the crack of light beneath the door. Even before it opened, she could smell the books inside. They circled the room on tall oak shelves. Most of the books had thick brown covers and barrel-ribbed spines, all faded and scuffed like the old green carpet on the floor. When she sat on his lap and he opened one up, the musty smell grew sweeter, and she put her nose in the very crease to breathe the odor in. The pages were yellowed, especially at the edges, where she liked to run her fingers on the rough-cut paper. The print was very black, but sometimes the letter in the north-west corner was a brilliant red and ten times the normal size. Tiny men and women, wearing sheets that did not stay on well, sat on these letters, and vines and flowers curled as on a trellis.

Uncle Garth would read aloud. Sometimes Grace listened, and sometimes she just smelled, and sometimes she rubbed the ragged edges of the paper. But with each ponderous turn of the page, she always hunted for the big red letter. Once she saw a purple one, squealed, pounced on it. She often wondered what it would be like to wear flowers and sheets and sit on a letter in one of her uncle's books.

Uncle Garth read well. When the story had a giant in it, his voice rumbled, and she felt his stomach shudder. When there were fairies, she felt tiny moths that tickled her tongue. She had wanted to know how he did it. One day she asked.

"Ho ho!" he laughed, and she felt his stomach shudder in his giant's voice. He bent his face very close. "You can too," he whispered. "Just you and I, niece. It's who we are. And a wonderful thing too." She never forgot it, even though she wasn't sure exactly what he meant.

Although they lived in the same town, Grace received many letters from her uncle, and she dutifully answered them. He was careful to begin the first word after "My Dearest Grace" with a large red capital, all bestrewn with marmots and wild strawberry vines. Grace always began her reply with the same red letter, carefully copied from the one he had drawn. He began with a different one each time, so that in just a few years they had run through the entire alphabet. *X* had been a problem, of course, but he had addressed the subject of xylophones, and she Xmas (which was cheating, a little).

When Grace entered junior high school, she left off copying the large red letters. Her replies became more brief, more general, more delayed. In the eighth grade, she moved with her parents to another city and began to subscribe to a magazine that advertised lip gloss and eye shadow on almost every page. It was then that she quit answering her uncle's letters altogether, and before very long she only heard from him on birthdays. And since her parents did not like to visit Garth, she was happily spared the awkwardness of seeing him.

Now, however, Grace missed her uncle. She sighed as she looked at the poem on her lap. And then a pleasant thought occurred. If she could not find her way to the road, perhaps she could find Uncle Garth. The wilderness surely was not that large. She *might* run into him.

Just then she heard footsteps—footsteps thumping the hollow earth on the trail below. Might it be? Even now? She peeked around the trunk, flattening her cheek to the bark. Hope sprang, only to be sprung: Garth it was not. Instead she saw the red-bearded leader with Lance on his heels. They marched quickly, wearing only rucksacks. Their eyes swished back and forth like searchlights.

Grace ducked behind the tree and pressed her back against the trunk. She sat holding her knees to her chin. Her head felt light again. When the footsteps were passing directly beneath her, it was Lance's voice she heard. "Hey, like—can we stop a minute?"

The footsteps ceased. "Sure," said the leader.

Twigs began to snap. It took just a few seconds for Grace to realize that hers was the largest tree by the trail. She braced herself. The first thing she saw when he rounded the trunk was his belt hanging loose. On impulse she grabbed it and hauled him down beside her before he could say "no kidding?"—which he said a little later.

"One word and you've had it," she hissed. She was not at all sure what it was he would have.

"No kidding?" he said. His eyes bulged out like toadstools.

"I mean it," she whispered. They regarded each other warily, deadlocked in threat and surprise. This status quo might well have persisted had they not heard the sound of another pair of footsteps. The footsteps stopped directly below them.

"Howdy." That was the leader, pretending to be Wyatt Earp.

There was no reply.

"Say, maybe you could help me out. Have you seen a girl on the trail, sixteen or so? Long brown hair, sort of tanned, orange pack?"

Sort of tanned? Grace wondered. *Sort of?*

A pause, then a voice. "What's the name?" She knew the voice. It belonged to the man from the end of the trail.

"Grace. Grace Foster. I know, it's a funny name."

What's so funny about it? Grace wanted to know.

There was another pause down on the trail.

"No," came the voice finally. "Haven't seen her."

"I don't believe it," Grace whispered to herself. Then she included Lance. "I don't believe it," she said aloud. "Bizarre."

"Who is?" said Lance.

"Quiet!" she ordered. "They'll hear you."

"No more than they'll hear you," he replied.

That took her aback. The only defiant person she liked was herself.

"What are you doing here?" Lance pressed. "Why'd you split? Couldn't take it? Home to mama?"

Grace shrugged her shoulders.

He leaned towards her. "We were supposed to go climbing today. Why did you ruin it?" The anguish in his voice carried well beyond the tree.

"Everything coming out all right up there?" called the leader. He cackled wickedly.

Grace recovered herself and nodded towards the laughter. "So," she said, "you call that a good time?" She paused dramatically.

Lance thought it over. There was something curious in the way he looked at her.

"You like this boot-camp stuff, Lance? You call this trip fun?"

Lance thought about it some more. Rhetorical questions

always stunned him. That and the sound of his name on female lips. "Uh, I—"

She cut him off with a fierce whisper. "Listen, you don't think it takes a little machisma to hike all night?" She paused to gauge the effect of her question. "Don't give me this bit about 'home to mama.' I can be tough when I want to be tough. See, I've been up here lots of times all by myself. But if you think I'm going to follow some red-bearded peacock around in the woods for a week and a half, you can guess again, buddy."

This came off well. Lance looked impressed with her patched-up tale. "So you're still planning to get away?" he asked blandly.

"No doubt about it," she affirmed. She felt more doubtful every minute.

There was a long pause.

"Well," he said, "I think I know why you left. That guy—he, like, never tells you anything you want to know, and he tells you lots of things you don't want to know." Here Lance pulled from his pocket a small roll of toilet paper. "But he don't know everything."

Grace could not help smiling.

"And those other ones." He rolled his eyes. "Two of them—those two boys—aren't even supposed to be on this trip. They're too young—they're junior high. Their parents talked somebody into letting them come."

"I thought so," said Grace.

"And that one girl," said Lance. "She's like, so *mellow*." He lingered on the word derisively. "It just kills me. This morning she asked what my sign was."

They shared a good sneer.

"And those other two girls," Grace went on. "Did you hear them last night? They asked him five times if there were any bears."

They both snickered as if to say, "Imagine. Afraid of bears!" Then another silence ensued. They had run out of persons to critique, except for each other, and there would be plenty of time for that perhaps.

"Would you mind," began Lance, "if, um . . ." His whisper had grown throaty. "I mean, would you mind if I like, went with you?"

Grace tried to appear indifferent. "I don't know," she pondered aloud. "You got a map? Did you bring any food?"

"Both right here," he said eagerly. He pointed at the rucksack on his back.

She still looked dubious. "Can you make yourself useful? Clean my boots? Cook supper? Light my pipe?"

"Shee-it!" said Lance. He began to laugh.

"What, Lance?" called the leader.

"Nothing," he shouted. "Down in a minute. I'm looking for some smooth stones."

"So was David," said Grace, unable to suppress herself.

"David who?" said Lance.

"Douglas fir cones," shouted the leader. "They're good when they're wet."

Lance peeked around the tree trunk. "The other guy's gone," he whispered.

"We should be too," Grace said. "Help me with the pack."

Lance hoisted it up. Grace slid her arms through the straps as if slipping into coat sleeves.

"We've got to crawl for a while," she told him. "Don't break any sticks."

Hunched over like two slavish courtiers groveling towards an Oriental despot, they left the cedar tree and inched into the woods. It was hard to crawl noiselessly—the bushes rattled like tambourines.

In a short while they heard a voice: "Lance! Lance, where are you? Lance?"

They looked behind them. The cedar tree was no longer visible.

"Let's walk," said Lance. "If we run, he might hear us."

They rose and tiptoed through mats of salal, holding their breath, pantomiming agility itself. The calling voice echoed more faintly as they went, and soon they heard it not at all. That was sweetest silence.

And so they walked till they came to a stream deep in the forest. The water looked a very dark green in the shade. The stream was not so swift or so deep that they could not cross, but they felt safe for the time being, not to mention clever, so they took off their packs on the mossy bank and drank their fill. The water was strangely tepid. Chins dripping, they scooted back and sat side by side in the sloping moss. Grace pulled out the disemboweled apple, took a bite, and offered it to Lance. He ate the rest.

In the quiet, they knew: there was no leader, no group, no stranger on the trail—just the two of them. The nakedness of it began to sink in. The silence turned shy. The dark current slid quietly past, and a black whirlpool eddied at their feet. A toad they had not seen beside them plopped into the water.

Lance gathered his courage. He looked Grace full in the face. She looked away. Then before he had given the order, his hand began creeping along the moss—secretly behind her back—like a large but discreet spider. Before it reached her, she sat up straight and put her hands in her lap.

"What stream is this?" she urgently asked. "Look at your map! Who's got a map? Everybody should know what they have!"

They both laughed, but not spontaneously. Lance reached dutifully into his rucksack and unfolded the square green map with white borders. Some of the folds were starting to tear, and the borders were already smudged. He had to consult it only briefly.

"This should be Lira Creek."

"How do you know?"

"It's the next one north of the stream by the trail. We've contoured almost a mile."

She grabbed his hand and saved him all his sneaking effort.

"Lance, the trail you came down today—is it the very same one we hiked up yesterday?"

"Of course."

"You're sure?"

"I'm sure. There's no other trail, not below the meadows anyway."

Grace looked slack-jawed at the dark eddy. "Bizarre," she said.

"Who is?" asked Lance.

5

IT TOOK MUCH EXPLAINING on Grace's part, but Lance finally believed her, or at least said he did—to preserve the savor of their new acquaintance. He foresaw them wandering arm in arm through forests and sunsets, their lips shyly meeting in the glimmering twilight, and not so shyly meeting after dark. Let the highway be gone. Her earnestness on this point scared him a little, but only enough to tinge infatuation with the exotic. He would go along with her plans—until the gorp ran out, anyway.

Her plans were to find Garth.

"Where did the guy say he would meet him?" asked Lance. He was picking the chocolate chips from his stash. Most of them were already gone. All he could find were peanuts and raisins.

"On the other side of the mountain," said Grace.

"Which one? There's three of 'em, y'know." He held up three raisins by way of illustration.

"He didn't say," she meekly answered.

"That's easy then," he said. "We just hop on over to the other side of *the* mountain and chance upon your long-lost uncle." He laughed.

Grace did not. She used the moment to ponder his possible imperfections. "Well, which mountain does the trail go to?" she asked.

Lance checked the map. "South Queen." Why hadn't he thought of that?

"There you go," said Grace. She blessed him with a satisfied smile. "And there *we* go. Let's find a way to the other side of the South Queen. And who knows? Maybe there are roads on that side. If we don't find my uncle, I bet we can still get out of this place."

This sounded plausible to Lance, so together they consulted the map, or rather Lance consulted the map, and Grace looked vaguely over his shoulder.

"Lira Creek ought to do it," he said. "It'll take us to the saddle between the South and Center Queen. From there we pop over to the other side."

Grace, who saw only a morass of squiggly lines, readily agreed.

By now it was early afternoon. They got up stiffly, put on their packs, and peered at the dark forest. It looked nothing at all like the green piece of paper they had spread on the moss. The map had been so cozy. You slid your finger across the paper, and you were there. Standing up in the forest was different. The problem was, you *were* there.

Lance had his own way of coping — he gallantly offered to take Grace's pack. Grace replied that she could carry her own pack quite well, thank you, to which Lance responded that he was just as capable and more than willing, to which Grace answered that if she wanted him to take her pack she would ask, to which Lance replied that she didn't have to be so touchy, at which point Grace asked who was being touchy.

In this harmony of spirit they set out. And to their surprise, the forest quickly opened on a bright clearing. The sunlight raised their eyes and hopes. Over the treetops they spied the summit of the South Queen herself. It seemed quite close—a little walking, a little effort, and they would be past it.

Lance was first to notice the bushes hung with purple-blue berries. The berries filled the clearing. He stooped and picked one. It was the size of a pea.

"Think it's poisonous?" he asked.

She didn't know.

He placed it on his tongue.

"Good," he said. "Awesome!" It dawned on him there were more to be had. "Look at this mother! No. Here! Loads of 'em!"

They were huckleberries, and before long they were cascading one after the other into his mouth. Like a faithful retriever, he passed his better prizes on to Grace, but she let them slip through her fingers when he wasn't looking, which was most of the time. She had noticed the spreading purple stain that graced his lips and tongue. The effect was not handsome.

When Lance had gorged himself, they again set out. The stream led them into the forest once more, and soon they came to a desperate thicket of slide alder. The alder trunks shot everywhere in slippery layers, ready to slap, to trap, to crush the unwary—an arboreal Slough of Despond. Fools rush in, and so did Grace and Lance. Grace bravely barked her shins and knees in all the same places that she had the night before—which might have been tolerable if she were getting somewhere. But no sooner did her foot cross one small trunk than another knocked her back. Pairs of branches closed on her waist like wooden scissors. Other times they pinned her pack frame firmly in place.

The time came to get serious. She lashed, she cursed, she trampled, she swore, she heroically unleashed a branch directly into Lance's face. It caught him with a vicious swat. He stifled a response, but reflected that the magic moments they so recently had shared were perhaps forever ended. He saw that Grace's hair had filled with twigs and leaves. Greasy locks lay plastered on her sweat-streaked forehead. It came as a revelation: she was not that beautiful after all.

After an hour of this pastime, the thicket was as thick as ever. Every so often Grace asked if this were the best way, and Lance replied each time that they could go back the way they had come if she wanted, and each time Grace declined.

But at last, when the alder had whipped their patience to a raw and bleeding spectacle, the thicket vanished. Before them, the creek ran languidly between dark pools set in a wide space of moss. Neither Grace nor Lance had ever seen moss so soft, so smooth, so green, so inviting. Spaced across the carpeted expanse, like potted palms in a hotel lobby, grew head-high plants with huge green leaves. They had stumbled on paradise.

"We're finally out of that stuff," said Grace. She looked at Lance in a way that held him fully responsible for "that stuff."

"Don't blame me," he said.

"Who's blaming you?"

She was being insupportable, and she knew it. So what happened next should have been no surprise. Brushing the leaves and twigs from her arms, she set off in a huff. Her feet hit the moss—and sank like millstones. Wet black ooze poured over her boot tops. She mentioned this to Lance: "Laaance!" For his part, Lance had never seen anything quite so amusing. He laughed drunkenly on the dry shore.

The muck clung cold and thick around her ankles. She pulled up hard on her right foot. It slowly surfaced, then pulled free with a loud black suck. The wet ooze gushed and gurgled in the footstep. Her foot now hovered in air, dripping its mantle of sludge on the moss. For a moment Grace felt the domestic horror of turning around in a living room to see the mud she had tracked on the carpet. But her problems were much deeper. In regards to her left leg, about knee-deep.

"Help me!" she wailed. "I mean it, Lance."

Lance lost control. Laughter convulsed him like a demon.

Grace grabbed wildly at the stalk of a nearby plant, one of the many so tastefully spaced across the green. It happened to be devil's club; her hand closed tight upon hundreds of needles. "Aiiee!" she cried, and drew back her hand. The flesh was all prickled with hairlike spines. They burned without mercy. Her palm began throbbing in red and white splotches. Meanwhile, she had planted her right foot beneath the moss again, and now both legs were stuck fast.

Lance roared.

"You pig!" she shouted. "You filthy pig! Get me out of here!"

Because her back was toward him, she had to twist around awkwardly to deliver her withering stare. And, more intent on executing the gaze of revenge than on keeping her balance, she collapsed in the mire with an ungainly shriek. Lance stopped laughing.

"So you finally realize this is serious," said Grace. She was reclining in the ooze at his feet.

There was no reply.

"Here's my hand," she offered.

She saw then that Lance was not looking at her. He was watching something across the bog. His mouth hung open. Grace turned and looked too. And gasped.

Wending their way across the mossy expanse were four pair of marmots harnessed in a column to a small barge. To Grace, who had never before seen a live marmot, they looked a little like cats—or perhaps beavers. Unlike Grace, they were light enough apparently to stay atop the moss. In the front of the barge a single silvered marmot was standing upright, holding the reins between his paws. Behind him, seated on a high-backed chair, was the most imposing woman Grace had ever seen. The woman wore a long gown of the brightest red. Her raven hair swept both bare shoulders. She held her head high and rested her hands on the arms of the chair with great composure. The skin of her face was white and firm, and her eyes were green and dark and direct. The barge was slowly winding towards Lance and Grace; the eyes of the lady were fixed upon them with cool interest. Soon the team of marmots drew up beside them and stopped at the edge of the bog.

"Stuck, I see," the woman announced. Her voice rang high overhead in the tree boughs. "Perhaps the young man could be of assistance." Lance was skewered with a commanding stare.

He looked back dumbly, his mouth still open.

"Hop to it, boy," she said. "Stop your flycatching."

As if in a trance, Lance reached down to Grace's hand. He began to pull. It took both of his hands and both of hers before she moved at all. The bog around her shuddered like pudding; her legs began to slip out like spoons retrieved from the very bottom of a bowl. Lance strained, his teeth clenched manfully. When least expected, her feet popped free, and both of them tumbled onto the bank. The bog regurgitated noisily in her footsteps.

"Splendid, young man. Splendid," said the lady.

Lance's face showed a shy tinge of heroism, but Grace looked down at her filthy legs in distress. "My boots are gone," she cried. "I've lost my boots." She had only a very muddy pair of wool socks on her feet.

"So you have," said the woman. "And you are right—they really are lost."

Lance sat panting while Grace looked the woman in the eye. It scared her, but she had to try. She encountered flint hardness; the power there astonished her. The woman was eagerly looking for something.

"Let me introduce myself, weary travelers," said the woman. "I am Lady Lira, and my doorstep is near at hand. My house lies open to succor those who must cross these wastes. So allow me to beseech you. Look about—the day is far gone. Surely you are tired and in need of rest. Warm baths, hot meat, a pillow for your heads—will these not help you on your way?"

Grace, coated like a tar baby, heard the word *baths*. Lance, his chocolate chips depleted, heard the word *meat*.

"I get so few visitors in these desolate parts, and seldom does such a strong young man come to my door, or such a clever young lady with sparkling eyes."

Lance blushed, and Grace, though she recognized flattery when she heard it, visibly glowed. If anyone else had talked this way, Grace would have laughed aloud. But Lady Lira had bizarre authority.

"You will come then," she said. "Here, there is room on the barge at my feet."

Lance and Grace exchanged a glance, not to consult, but to share their awe.

"Don't be frightened," said Lady Lira. "I won't eat you." She laughed at the thought.

Lance slipped nervously onto the barge and crouched at her feet. He did not need to crouch, but it felt appropriate. Grace still hung back. On second thought, she did not like the reference to her sparkling eyes.

"Is the young lady bashful?" asked Lady Lira. "I have extra shoes at home. You are welcome to any pair you like. Come now. Be bold like your companion."

Lance, who looked anything but bold, blushed once more. He could not keep his eyes off of her.

"It's not that," Grace lied. "It's just that I don't want to get any mud on your beautiful dress."

"Oh!" trilled Lady Lira. "Take no thought for that. I have so many more at home, and one for you too, after your bath."

Grace was just vain enough to picture herself in Lady

Lira's shoes and in her gown too, sweeping through forests and sunsets in bare-shouldered glory. She would be stunning. So she stepped onto the barge, stood before the chair, and shrugged her pack onto the deck. It lay upside down in its own filth, helpless as a potato bug.

"That's it, dear. Now we must all become better acquainted. I have told you my name. I pray you, tell me yours."

"I'm Lance." It was the first he had spoken.

"Grace," said Grace.

"Splendid," said Lady Lira. "Now we are properly introduced."

She looked past them now to the marmot before her. All this time he had quietly stood at the helm of the barge. Grace, in fact, had already felt the urge to stroke his head.

"James," said Lady Lira, "home." The marmot jiggled the reins before him, and the barge slid away across the moss, slowly weaving through spiny clumps of devil's club.

The leaves of poison slipping by made Grace remember that her hands were still on fire. She was cold and muddy. And she couldn't help feeling a little frightened of Lady Lira. But at the same time, she laughed inside that anyone would have a driver—a furry one, no less—to whom she would say, "Home, James."

6

HE SHOULD HAVE KNOWN. Something in her eyes. Was she granddaughter, cousin, niece to the old man? The moment William heard her name, he knew he must find Grace in the wilderness. So he told the red-bearded one he had not seen her and went on his way. The red-bearded fellow presumably went his.

Yesterevening still grew on him. He remembered flinging the pack off, trampling the ferns, snatching the fronds till his palms ran green—then rioting in the underbrush, crashing in the alder, tearing limb from limb until darkness came. Given a machete, William would have put a whole trail crew to shame. But there was no trail to be cleared—not even a deer path. That was the big surprise.

And the dreams he had had, there in that misplaced field of ferns—ravens hurtling, ice worms wriggling, axes swinging in radiant fog. Then a dark forest tide had swept out before him, sucking at his knees. It regathered itself in a great green wave, piling up against the horizon, heap upon heap. He turned and ran for the mountaintop, but a terrible rainbow crowned the summit, an emerald rainbow too stunning to look upon. So he turned again to the mounting wave. It smashed in upon him, tumbling him down into deep green chaos; then he awoke, sodden with dew, the scent of fern like oil on his brow, and a waning moon in the fronds overhead.

In the morning Grace had come and gone. Why had he been so smug with her? Why had he bullied her off? He could not say. He only knew he was lonely when she left.

William, in fact, had never felt so small in the forest. At all other times, the woods were but a thin strip of green between a parked car and a mountaintop, easily crossed in a scramble to a high camp, easily recrossed in a dash to a hot shower. He had always ignored it without effort. But now the forest was large enough to ignore him. A tide pool had spread itself into an ocean, not something to splash through but something to drown in. Unfathomed acres pressed in on his shoulders. He could hardly bear it. Which is why he had come back up the trail. He had to escape the forest in a way that a child must escape a dark closet. The weight of darkness suffocates, and so can the green weight of glory.

Of course, he had also come back up the trail because high in the meadows was a junction. At the end of another trail, perhaps, he would find a road. But that he doubted. Garth's windspoken disappearance howled in his mind. The man—gone; the road—gone; the forest—here and everywhere. It was all too strange and tied together. He had a key. He had a poem. The key might unlock something. So might the poem. But the poem itself needed unlocking. He wished for someone who could read it better than he could. This much he had known by the time that he met the man with the red beard.

Now he knew more. He knew he needed Grace. So William walked on, at each bend hoping to catch a glimpse of the girl with the orange pack. But Grace eluded him.

And soon, weary of crisis, his mind took rest in the ordinary. Today was Monday, and he should have been at work. On Mondays, William enjoyed telling people at the office about his weekends. He especially liked to tell his supervisor. He would wander to her door and slouch against the frame with a mug of coffee in hand. His slouch showed how fatigued he must be, and displayed the casual indifference of an outdoorsman toward the confines of a mere office building.

On the Monday before, his supervisor had smiled and asked, "How was your weekend, William?"

"Pretty good," he had answered. "I went to the mountains."

"Oh? Where?"

"You ever been up around Jackass Lake?"

"Jackass Lake," she told herself. She looked for the lake in the cracks of her fingernail polish. "Is that the one you drive by on the pass?"

"No," he replied. "You can't drive to it. You have to hike in."

"Oh my," she said. "So you walked the whole way. How far was it?"

"To the lake, you mean? About four miles is all."

"Four miles is quite a bit for an old lady like me!" She laughed explosively. "Was the fishing good?"

"No," said William. "I mean, I don't know. I didn't go fishing."

"Mm," she replied. Her eyes began scanning the memos for the morning on her computer screen.

"I was doing a little climbing," William added.

She looked back up, and William saw her eyes widen. "Oh, that's right," she gushed. "I'd forgotten. You're our mountain climber! You be careful up there, William."

"It's very safe, really, if you know what you're doing," William said. He scuffed his toe against the door frame modestly.

Now, as he walked through the forest, William's hand still gripped his coffee cup. The other hand made casual gestures. Sometimes his shoulders shrugged beneath the red tower of his pack, and sometimes his lips moved silently. It was more pleasant on a Monday to talk in the office than to walk in the mountains.

At length the trail broke into the meadow. The gleaming South Queen hove upwards once more. He stopped. Still he had not found Grace. He glanced at his watch and found it had halted at the eleventh hour—there was no clock in the forest.

Out of habit, he looked up and raked the peak with a hungry eye. The easy snowfield they had climbed was on the right. On the left, more to William's taste, a glacier tumbled down steep blue steps, each step splintered in jagged seracs. A lava headwall, bright red, rose above the cirque of the glacier. William could not tell for sure, but he thought he saw a ribbon of ice that split the headwall clear to the summit. Would it go? He eyed the tiny summit horns and locked his gaze in the gun sight between them. Even as he watched, a white cloud tip poked into the slot.

"Quiet!" said a voice. William heard giggles in the grass behind him.

"Look at that pack!" said another.

William turned around. Just off the trail were two young boys lying on their stomachs before a small burrow.

"Shut up! Shut up!" said one to the other. "He hears us, he sees us, he's coming."

They sat up as William approached. He asked if they had seen Grace. They hadn't, not since yesterday anyhow.

"Hey, mister," said one, "you ever climbed that mountain?"

"Yesterday," said William.

The boys exchanged looks of wonder.

"How hard is it?" asked the boy. He was wiggling his legs and picking at the grass.

The other boy cut in before William could answer. "Did he say we were gonna climb it? He didn't say for sure, did he?"

"I bet we will," said the first. "He'll probably make us do it."

"Looks scary to me," said the second.

"You chicken?" said the first.

"You said it looked scary yourself a minute ago," said the second.

"Like yeah," said the first boy scornfully.

The second boy appealed to William. "How scary is it?" The boy was pale and thin and wore black-framed glasses that made him look like a gangly raccoon. The other boy had swirls of freckles across his face, and red hair, cowlicked. They looked intently at William. A black wet nose poked out from the burrow behind them.

"It's not hard if you go up on the right," said William. He set his pack down to rest.

"I bet that's how we'll go," said the boy with the cowlick.

"Yeah," said the pale one, "but what's easy for him might not be so easy for us."

"Hey," said the first boy to William, "you ever caught a marmot?"

"No," said William. He saw the nose withdraw into the burrow.

"There's one in here," said the boy. "We're gonna catch him when he comes out."

They all looked at the hole.

"Hey, mister," said the freckled one, "want to see my blister?"

"You should see his blister," said the other. "Big as a half dollar."

The first boy took off his boot and peeled away several socks. The sock closest to the skin was bloody at the heel. Underneath was a glistening red sore. He twisted his foot so that William could see it in full. "Bet you never saw one that big," he said.

"Look out!" said the raccoon-faced boy. A silver blur charged out of the den. The boy lunged. He knocked it against his friend's bare foot and tried to hold its furry sides. "I got him!—I think. Gimme some help, Arnie!"

Arnie grabbed his foot and screamed. "He bit me! He bit me! Ronald, he bit me! My blister, it hurts! It hurts! It hurts!"

The marmot shrieked like an escaped balloon and shot into a lupine patch. There at a distance it sat up and whistled, one blast after another. Each series faded like a disappearing train.

"You can't believe how it hurts!" said Arnie. He held up his heel to solicit belief anyway. William stepped nearer to look. Blood welled out of two incised holes in the round red blister.

William's stomach began to tremble. "Best to let it bleed out," he told him.

Arnie looked pale between his freckles. "Who's got the first-aid kit?" he asked.

"How should I know?" said Ronald. He maneuvered in for a closer look. "Wow," he said reverently.

The boys, mesmerized, watched the blood drip. It fell from the heel and hung on separate blades of grass, wet, shining, a crimson dew upon the meadow. They were watching so closely that they merely heard a grassy thud.

Ronald glanced up. The man in red was stretched on the ground, his head softly pillowed in a blazing clump of Indian paintbrush. How peaceful he looked.

7

RONALD AND ARNIE NO sooner saw the man prostrate than they made bloody tracks to their camp across the meadow. Now more than ever they needed the first-aid kit. Surely it contained some potion to revive the faint or to raise the dead. Once in camp they tossed through mounds of sleeping bags and piles of nylon clothing. They ransacked a row of slump-sided packs leaned up against a log.

"It's in a red bag, right?" said Ronald.

"Hey," said Arnie. "Where's the first-aid kit?"

He was addressing three girls lying on foam pads behind the log. They all wore shorts, and their tee-shirts were rolled up to their navels. Each played shepherdess to an enormous flock of mosquitoes.

"Got him!" said one girl, slapping her stomach.

"You've got it?" said Ronald.

"Got what?"

"Forget it," said Arnie. "Here it is."

He leaned over the log and snatched a red bag from beside the girls' heads. It was open, and scissors and moleskin scraps poured into the dust unnoticed. Arnie and Ronald stirred through the remaining contents. A roll of dirty white tape first caught their eye, and they decided to bandage Arnie's heel before looking any further. The tape, however, was impossible to sever. Each strip wrinkled to a gummy knot as they tried to tear it from the roll. The scissors, of course, lay safely hidden behind the log.

"Forget it," said Arnie. "It probably needs to air out anyway."

They recognized everything else in the kit except a sticky brown bottle labeled Tincture of Benzoin. Ronald held it up. Nothing else looked potent enough to arouse the stranger. But even as Ronald held the bottle aloft, the sun disappeared, and the meadow darkened round about them. The tiny white cloud at the tip of the mountain had spread like ripples on a black pond. Whitebark pine twigs started to quiver. The girls arose, picked up their pads, and climbed over the log. They rolled down their tee-shirts and joined the boys in staring at the sky.

"Think it'll rain?" asked Ronald. His voice was reverential. Indoors, the question would have sounded idle.

Just then a thunderclap sounded on high. The three girls screamed in unison, then tittered nervously. Ronald and Arnie kept silence, but old fear bellowed in their hearts. Then came a second blast, avalanching into the meadows like a bursting glacier.

Just that spring, Ronald had completed an earth science project on "What Makes Thunder?" It had won second prize in the eighth grade science fair. The thunder itself was represented by the red letters *BOOM!!* which he painted on the posterboard at the end of a series of diagrams. But now the thunder was gray and hollow and full of might. It echoed terribly between the mountains, and each rolling echo tumbled Ronald's poster across the treetops, shredding it upon silver snags, hurling the title into an eagle's nest: "What Makes Thunder?"

"It's raining, it's raining!" shouted the girls. Fat drops kicked up the dust at their feet.

"Who's got the tent?" the oldest girl yelled.

"We don't have a tent," said Ronald. "We have a rainfly." He quailed inside. He knew that the green nylon bundle in his pack was called a rainfly, but he had no idea how to set it up.

The rain came more earnestly, and the wind moaned.

"Put your ponchos on first," he told everyone. "Then help me set up the fly."

The words amazed him. He had never taken charge of a crisis in his life. The girls immediately donned their ponchos, and this amazed him more. People were doing things merely because he had told them to. He usually just did whatever Arnie suggested. But now Arnie was silent, stooped over, looking at his bloody heel. Arnie had not put on his poncho. Ronald found the poncho and threw it over him.

"You okay, Arnie?"

"I'm okay," he said quietly.

Ronald did not put on his own poncho. There wasn't time. He began to unwind a small rope from around the rainfly. The girls huddled in a row before him, cowled like wizards in their blue rain robes. Once the fly was unfolded, an intestinal mass of white cord emerged. Ronald knelt down like a diviner examining the entrails of a sacrificed animal. He found many separate cords all snarled together. Each was attached to a different point on the edge of the fly.

"Let's get these lines untangled," said Ronald.

"*BOOM*!!" went the thunder.

Obediently, the three girls knelt with him to unravel the great knot.

"Hey, don't. Don't pull that one."

"Wait a sec—I'm trying to get this end through."

"Here, let go."

"There, I got it."

"You just made it worse!"

"No, get that part."

"Stop! Look what you just did."

"What'd I do?"

Ronald grew scared. He could command ponchos into place, but he could not command the cord to disentangle. His shirt stuck wet on his back. He shivered.

Fortunately, nature and genius intervened.

"It's hailing!" screamed the girls. The meadow around them filled with a white hiss. Pellets sprang from the rainfly and rolled into the folds, piling up in little drifts.

"Let's just get it over us," one girl said. At once they abandoned the knot and crawled under the fly, using their heads and shoulders for tent poles. Arnie, still staring at his heel, had to be pulled inside. They sat cross-legged atop wet sleeping bags, facing each other in a tight circle. The hail seemed to bang on the fly even harder. But they had fenced it out, and blew their steamy breath into one another's faces.

Ronald was scrunched up against the oldest girl with long braids, the one who had gotten them under the fly. Her hand rested carelessly on his knee. He had never in his life been so close to a girl, but it seemed best to pretend that he had. His glasses had fogged up completely.

"Are you warm enough?" she asked him.

"Sure," said Ronald. His teeth began to chatter.

"Here," she said. "I've got an extra sweater in my pack."

As it happened, her pack was under the fly behind her, and she quickly gave the sweater to Ronald. It was pink, but he put it on. Under the fly it looked a little greenish, and that was some comfort. He wished he could remember her name.

Meanwhile, the girl turned her attention to Arnie. "How are you doing?" she asked.

"Fine," he said.

"Let me see your heel." She had noticed, though no one had told her.

Arnie stuck his heel in her lap, exposing the bitten blister.

"Gross!" said the other two girls.

Arnie looked numbly at the first-aid kit still clutched in his hand. He passed it over on demand. The girl washed his wound with a clear solution, then bandaged it with gauze and tape. The tape tore cleanly along her fingernails.

Ronald was just beginning to feel the warmth of wet wool, wet nylon, wet bodies stirred together. Then he remembered. "There's a man," he blurted. "Out on the meadow. He's unconscious or something. He's not moving." He wondered how he had forgotten.

"Are you kidding?" said the girl.

"He's not kidding," said Arnie. Now that his heel was bandaged he felt like talking again. He told them the whole story. When he had finished, they heard the hail beat the fly and felt it hit their heads. It made their silence loud.

"We should—go help him, shouldn't we?" said the girl. The prospect was fearful.

"We were going to bring him some—some . . ."

"Tincture of Benzoin," said Ronald.

"I think that's what my mother uses when she gets dizzy," said another of the girls. "She puts it in her ear with a eye-dropper."

"I don't think we have an eyedropper," said Ronald. He had an eye for detail.

"I think we should check on him anyway," said the first girl. She squeezed Ronald's knee for the second time. "Why don't you come with me? No use everybody going."

Ronald was electrified. Never before had he been asked out. "Sure," he said. His voice was breathless.

The girl grabbed the first-aid kit with one hand and Ronald's arm with the other. Together they peeled off their side of the fly and stood up in the hail. It did not feel as terrifying as it had sounded. The slick green fly, draped over the others, quivered on the ground like a lump of lime gelatin.

"Which way?" she asked.

Ronald found his poncho and dutifully led her toward the trail. They walked silently for a hundred yards, drenching their knees and calves in the grass. The hail ricocheted off their shoulders. Then, curiously, they stepped out of the hail as if through a curtain. Around them the air hung still. Beside them the hail fell hissing. They could have been standing by a waterfall.

"How funny," said the girl.

"The sun!" said Ronald.

Suddenly its beams were pouring under the clouds. The meadow glowed an astonishing green. For an instant the curtain of hail shone white beside them, transfigured to a brighter splendor. Then it simply melted from the sky, and the black clouds glistened in a new stillness. In the stillness they heard toads and frogs—croaking, croaking at the death of the hail,

As if there were no such cold thing.

"A rainbow!" said the girl.

It arched from a snowfield, crossed the sky, and dropped into the dripping forest. The mountain hemlocks bloomed like roses, like daffodils, like violets. This end of the rainbow was not far away; it touched where the trail emerged from the forest. The boy and the girl hurried on toward the rainbow's end and breathed the wet air, new-bathed with light. They strained to gather in the rainbow—all of it, all at once.

They were almost to the forest when Ronald held up his hand and stopped. "He was right here. There's the marmot hole." He pointed at it.

"The same one?"

"Yep." He paused. "Pretty sure."

"Well, he's not here now," she observed.

A horrible thought struck Ronald. *What if the man had*

been dragged away and eaten by marmots? It would not do to alarm the girl. He put a brave face on it: "I bet he just fainted, and the hail woke him up and he hiked off. It's not like he was hurt or anything."

The girl pondered his theory. "I hope none of those marmots started gnawing on him," she said.

"Marmots?" he replied. "They only eat grass and stuff. Don't be silly."

The girl nodded slowly. Then, case dismissed, she changed the subject. "What's your name?" she asked. "I know we told each other our names yesterday, but I forgot yours."

"My name?" said Ronald. The request thrilled him. "My name is Ronald." He tried to pronounce it in an important way.

"My name's Jennifer," said the girl. "I'm telling you because I think you're afraid to ask."

"Me?" said Ronald. "I was just going to ask."

"Well, now you know."

"Yep," he said, "now I know."

What Ronald did not know, however, was what else to say. He searched the sky and found that the rainbow had faded. He searched his mind for a suitable topic of conversation, even for a suitable phrase unrelated to a definite topic. None came. Their man was gone, the storm over, their mission completed, the crisis passed. What was left to them in common? Jennifer stood with her head cocked to one side, apparently inclined to let him suffer. The awkward moment broadened to a painful silence; it deepened to an abyss of despair. With all of his heart, Ronald wished he could crawl into the burrow at his feet and escape the face of the earth—better the bloody fangs of an herbivore than the fatal poison of shame.

Then from an unexpected quarter rescue arrived. Out of the trees trod their red-bearded leader, his boots bespattered with mud. Ronald ran to him in joy, and Jennifer came close behind.

"Did you find her?" he asked.

"Did you find her?" she asked.

"Where's Lance?" they both said.

The leader eyed them mournfully, as if he were not happy to see them but knew that he must. His face was scratched, his beard full of twigs. "We found her," he assured them. "Everything's fine. Grace got lost in the woods last night and sprained her ankle pretty bad. I had Lance drive her down to the hospital. We'll have to continue without them for a while."

He paused. "Any of the rest of you planning to run off on me?"

They shook their heads obediently.

"Why did she leave?" asked Jennifer. "Did she say?"

"Why did Lance have to go?" asked Ronald. "Why didn't you go?"

"Well, somebody's got to lead this trip," he snorted. He ignored Jennifer's question with one of his own: "So, staying out of trouble? I'll bet you guys figured out how to set up the rainfly in a hurry!" He laughed very loudly, as if it were a joke they were not supposed to get.

"We're doing fine," said Jennifer.

"Great," said Ronald.

On the way back to camp the two of them stayed well behind the leader. Jennifer tugged on Ronald's poncho and cupped her hand to his ear. "I'm glad she's gone," she whispered. "She was sort of a bitch."

8

Whence these red-bearded lies?

Whither William's body?

First, the beguiled instructor. When Lance did not come from the cedar tree, our leader went to check on him. Finding the spot empty, he wildly tore at the bark with his nails and beat upon his breast, cursing the day he had first signed on with You-Can-Do-It Expeditions. He called out Lance's name and searched the nearby woods, but all for naught. He had no birds in hand, and two in the bush.

Were the two birds together and taking flight to the trailhead? He feared so, and this was bitter for him. No one ever before had escaped from one of his trips. It was enough to make him wonder if the forest were enchanted. But the woods seemed as unenchanted as ever. They were simply his workplace, where he made people hoist heavy packs and back down cliffs and get up early in the morning. He had loved the wilderness once, and he thought he still did, but more and more he merely loved new ways to teach ice-ax technique, new "initiative tests" for the uninitiated, new rules of "minimum impact" to impose with maximum vigilance. More than he loved wilderness, he loved the idea of himself as a wilderness leader. That is why it hurt to see his leadership refused.

So, feeling disconsolate, he returned to the trail and hiked the remaining distance to the road. For him the road was once the outer boundary of adventure. But it too was part of his workplace now. It was the place where he met and disposed of his charges. Road or trail—it felt the same to him.

At the highway he saw no sign of Lance or Grace. But sitting by the waterfall was a bald man with a white beard. He offered the leader a cup of cold water. "Drink up," the old man told him. He did. It tasted more delicious than water ever had.

He asked the man how long he had been there.

"All my life, feels like." The old man guffawed.

Had he seen a girl and a boy hike out?

"Seems to me just half an hour ago," he said. "No sooner hit the pavement than they're waggling their thumbs, and wasn't five minutes till they got a ride down the mountain."

He asked what they looked like.

"The young fella—curly in the head, wearin' a rucksack. She had a full pack—orange, I think. Nice legs but chewed up by the skeeters." He guffawed again.

Was the old man going out?

"Outgoing anyways."

Would he deliver a note to the You-Can-Do-It Expeditions base camp down the road?

"I'll get it to the right place," he said.

So the leader wrote a note for the chief instructor, explaining that two students had escaped his strict supervision, and he entrusted the note with the white-bearded, bald old man. Then he began the long walk back to the meadows—long enough to concoct the tale which he told to Ronald and Jennifer. To the chief instructor he had to tell as much as half the bitter truth; he wished to save face with those left in his power.

Now, William, collapsed in the paintbrush. There he lay. Ants soon fell to exploring his armpits, and two mosquitoes delicately pierced his nose and drank their fill, gorging their pin-striped abdomens almost to the bursting point. They reeled away in sodden flight, and William awoke. His nose was throbbing, large as an apple. He felt for the escaped culprits, and then dove his hands for the armpit ants. He looked about at the empty meadow, at the empty burrow. Ah, he remembered. Yes, he was shaky still. But best to leave before rescue came. So he lurched to his feet, lifted his pack, and set out once again.

His trail climbed half a mile higher in the meadows, at times disappearing under sun-cupped snowbanks. At the very foot of the South Queen, the path reached a junction. Here he had camped with Garth. When he got there this time, the sky had darkened. He could turn left and traverse high meadows to the Center Queen, or turn right and dip into a web of wooded canyons to the south. He stood and pondered. Before he could decide, a thunderclap split the air, and he flinched. More thunder exploded. And more. Suddenly the choice gained cosmic proportions. How to decide? William had had enough of forests. He turned left.

As soon as he did so, a spate of rain thumped his chest. Thunder burst, the ground shook. Marmots mingled desperate whistles with wailing winds. All at once—and he had no idea why—William felt every inch a hero. His crimson coat flapped bravely about him; his bitten nose throbbed wildly in the rain. He strode the high trail like a giant in a tempest, not even bothering to walk around the swelling puddles of snowmelt. Rain became hail, and he firmly crushed the little balls of ice beneath his feet. The path, a gleaming white ribbon in the grass, uncoiled before his every step.

Thus he braved the elements till, having forgotten to don his gaiters, his boots filled up with hailstones. That was cold. Also, a widening rip in the nape of his hood had invited the hail onto his neck. Ice was dripping down his back, and that was very cold. William fell to unheroic bouts of shivering. He searched the land for shelter.

To his left, the meadow gave onto a rocky plateau, flecked with shining obsidian. The plateau halted at a lava rim and dropped away to the forest. To his right, the meadow rose through lava bluffs to moraines of glistening rubble. In the nearest outcrop, partially screened by a clump of trees, he spied a shadowed hollow beneath an overhang—perhaps a cave, at least a sheltered nook. It was worth checking into. He left the trail and drenched his sagging socks in the grass. His boots made sloshing, sucking noises, easily heard above wind and hail.

He reached the base of the overhang and pulled back branches of scrubby hemlock to get a closer look. It was a cave indeed, a lava tube, from the looks of it—a hollow conduit through which magma had once poured from mountain depths. He squirmed through the screen of snapping twigs and crouched in the tunnel entrance. It was dry, even quiet—he had left the hail behind. Off came the pack, off came the boots. He unrolled his mattress on little lava spikes and unleashed his bag in a shivering frenzy. There. Inside its crumpled folds, he found a dank and hazy warmth.

The hail ceased, the sun shone, the rainbow bent across his threshold. But William did not know. He lay surrounded by steaming clothes, snoring in the cave mouth, tucked away in a land of shadows.

9

GRACE WAS IN HEAVEN. The smoking water lapped to her very chin, and she lay half-floating in sponged indolence. The bath was huge. The basin itself was inlaid with tile, all a green mosaic save one red dragon couched on the bottom. The head of the dragon lay under Grace's heels, and out of its mouth boiled an underwater fountain that soothed her feet. Above her toes the water poured out through a notch in the brim. Thence it was channeled across the floor to a hole in the wall. All of the mud had sloughed off and drained away long ago. The water was clean now, and so was Grace. But she made no plans to get out. There was no better place to think.

Lady Lira's home was cavernous. After traveling a great distance across the green bog, they had come in the barge to a tall lava cliff. Here the bog ended. Or here it began, rather, for out of a cave flowed a murky sludge, the undistinguished headwaters of Lira Creek. Grace feared they would enter the cave itself. But at the very last instant, James pulled on the reins, and the barge veered left alongside the cliff. They slipped quietly beneath the face, so close to it that ferns on the cliffside trailed their fronds in Grace's hair. A vault of conchoidal obsidian passed, smooth and black, glinting like glass. Then they skirted the base of a fall that shot from a hole in the rock. The waterfall steamed; it sent hot spray upon their cheeks. And then the barge stopped. They were next to a rock landing that jutted out from a wooden door. There were window niches in the cliff above.

Grace had studied the door in the rock. It seemed an odd place to live. It seemed a strange sort of woman that lived here—dressed to kill and enthroned, imperious, on a marmot-drawn bogsled. Perhaps Lady Lira was merely eccentric. Perhaps she was the ranger's wife, and this was how she coped with boredom. Perhaps—but here Grace's hypotheses were shattered in thunder. Echoes crossed the hollow sky. The air thickened in new darkness.

"Quickly now," said Lady Lira. "Inside before it rains. Hurry—James will get your packs." She swept them over the landing and through the door, from gloom into gloom.

Inside was no ranger station. They traversed a dim passage and stopped on the edge of a great hall, carved deep in the rock. Its ceiling was lost in shadows. Long red hangings draped the walls, and torches sputtered in brackets. At the far end was a long table set crosswise. Behind it, two doors framed a huge lava fireplace. A glaring fire burned there now—Grace saw the table in silhouette against it.

She and Lance were standing on flagstones in the entry, but a thick green carpet spread out at their feet. In the center of the carpet was the immense woven figure of a red dragon. The creature was really too bloated for a dragon, but Grace knew no better name for it.

Lady Lira appeared from behind them. "Welcome home," she announced. Her voice echoed to the dark ceiling. Immediately a pair of marmots bounded towards them over the carpet.

"Baths for the guests!" she ordered.

The marmot next to Grace stood quickly up on his hind feet. He had silvered shoulders and a dusky face—and so looked a little like an overweight Siamese cat. But his buck teeth belonged to a beaver and his thick red tail to a raccoon.

The marmot pointed his nose in the air and squinted up at Grace. He squinted as if he had just awakened and could not find his glasses. Then he put his black-webbed paws on his belly and nodded politely. When Grace nodded back, the marmot collapsed on all four paws and darted off to a staircase. He dragged his tail like a limp rag, and at every step his shoulders quivered in furry rolls of fat. Grace followed, amused, and found her bath.

She lay there yet. The water soothed her swollen hand, the one poisoned by the devil's club. It gave her good enough reason to linger and to turn her thoughts to Lance. She saw him howling on the bank, his mouth a blackened cove in his face, his lips a purple stain. Had he lifted a finger to help her? He had not—not until ordered by Lady Lira. She saw him crouching on the barge, blushing obsequiously, gazing at the woman, adoring her bare shoulders. Just this morning, Grace had thought him emphatically cute. The memory of it brought wonder and disgust. So easily did one day turn the shadow of her judgment; so easily falls the son of the morning.

Right then, right there, Grace decided she could find her uncle on her own. There was firmness, there was satisfaction in her resolve. She raised her fist and thumped it squarely down in the bath—and shot a geyser into her eye. It did not faze her. She was invincible.

At this crux of glory her marmot reappeared. He stood upright in the doorway with a bundle in his paws. "Monsieur marmot," she asked, "can you help me find my uncle?" He walked unsteadily to the basin and held his burden up to Grace—on top, a red towel; underneath, a folded gray gown. But this trick of balance was too much to ask of a marmot. He swayed, he toppled, he crashed to the floor, and the laundry with him. Then up he shrieked, and he whistled out the door on all four feet.

Grace rose laughing from the water. "He just—he just—fell—over!" she sputtered. It put her into real merriment, enough to make her sides ache.

She stepped out, retrieved the towel and, having dried herself, put on the gray gown. A full-length mirror gave the proper prospect. At first Grace admired what she saw in the glass. But then a smile crossed the reflection of her face. The mirror, no less than the marmot, had awakened her sense of the true ridiculous. Her image presented but a flimsy imitation of Lady Lira's grandeur. *Let the woman deck herself out,* she thought. *No need to pay her the homage of an ape.*

The dress fell in a rumpled heap. Grace plucked her muddy shorts from a bench and plunged them in the bath. Her sweater went in too. She could wear them wet and dry them by the fire. So she scrubbed them off, wrung them out, put them on, and stepped into the cold upstairs hallway. Her marmot awaited her there.

"Do you know," she asked, "how cute you are?" She tried to stroke his silver back, but he ran down the passage to another door, where he stood up and nodded. Grace followed and looked in. She saw her pack leaning against a small bed that was built into a casement window. A single candle burned on the window ledge. Outside, in bog and forest, it was nearly dark.

Then the marmot brushed her legs and led her downstairs to the green carpet in the cavernous hall. Her bare feet sank softly in the carpet. It was like walking in a thick lawn, newly mown. She was sorry it ended before they got to the table and the fire.

Lance was already standing by the fireplace. The mantle was higher than his head. He wore a billowy white shirt, provided no doubt by Lady Lira. He looked at the fire. He looked at the ceiling. He did not look at Grace.

"Greetings, Prince Charming."

"Please," said Lance.

"So where's your shining armor? There are dragons, you know—deeds to be done. What about that big fat sucker right on the rug? Now *there's* a menace."

Lance sulked and scowled and scuffed the hearth.

Grace was content to let him be. She stood as close to the fire as she dared and felt her clothes dissolve in steam. Her marmot was gone. She wished him back to rub against her legs. When her front became hot, she put her back to the fire; when her back became hot, she turned around again. After turning several times, she realized her mind was more at ease when she faced the hall with her back to the fire. The room had the large hollowness of a deserted coliseum, the emptiness of a theater when the audience has left. The absence of those who might fill the hall was itself a discomfiting presence. So Grace kept watch and saw the shadows flicker on the carpet. That was best.

She was thus absorbed when the doors flew open on either side of the fireplace. She whirled. Lady Lira swept from the left door, trailing a long green gown. A column of marmots bearing cups and plates and food and drink trooped in from the right. What timing! What effect! Grace looked at Lance. He was trying his best to appear very calm. His arms hung down like fire pokers.

"Welcome again, my guests," said Lady Lira. "I trust you have bathed well." She spoke so loudly that Grace checked again to make certain that they were the only ones there.

The woman looked at them carefully. "Young man, your shirt becomes you. But, Grace, did I not send you better clothes? Did that clumsy marmot drop them?"

"Oh, no," said Grace. "He brought the gown, Lady Lira. I just feel more comfortable in—in shorts."

Lance failed to control a snicker.

Lady Lira dug hard at Grace with her eyes. Each eyebrow

arched like the back of a cat. "Of course," she purred. "Whatever is most comfortable for you."

The marmots, meanwhile, laid out the supper by mounting the benches and raising each dish to the table. Four places were set, a pair on each side, directly before the fire. Two of the marmots ushered Lance and Grace to the seats beside the hearth. Lady Lira walked around the table and assumed a place across from Lance. Grace wondered who the fourth setting was for. Then James the marmot popped up next to his mistress. He stood gravely upright on the bench with no apparent difficulty. Grace noticed that his mantle of fur was hoarier than that of the other marmots.

The plates and utensils gleamed like silver, because they were. Heaping dishes of savory meat and bread and greens were waiting for them in the glare of the fire. James the marmot filled their cups with something steamy and red.

They fell to—Grace with care, Lance with abandon. He only regretted there was no ketchup, and said so. But even *sans* ketchup his plate was soon empty, and Lady Lira quickly passed the meat to him again. "You eat no more than a pika," she scolded.

Grace had never tasted flesh so sweet and so tender. Like Lance, she wanted more. But she was too sleepy. The hot bath, the warm fire, the steaming food—not to mention the miles of trail, salal, and alder—all conspired against her in a yawn she could not stifle. Her head began to nod. She jerked it to attention—a reflex nurtured in lectures and sermons of days gone by. It would not do to fall asleep at the table. But could she hope to last until Lance had finished? He had started now on a third helping. She watched his plate doggedly. When it was clean, Lance looked up eagerly. Grace heard Lady Lira's voice from very far away.

"Dessert will taste much better," she said, "if we renew our appetites with the tales of your adventures. You have surely seen much that bears the telling. And perhaps, in knowing the end of your journey, I may be of greater assistance."

"What's for dessert?" asked Lance.

"You shall soon know," said Lady Lira. "But I long to hear of your travels."

Lance discerned he must sing for the rest of his supper. So he plunged in. "We were on a You-Can-Do-It Expedition, see, where you do climbing and stuff. Except our leader and the others, they were definite losers. So Grace, she split the first night and went back to the road, except it wasn't there, or she got lost, or something. Then the leader took me to look for her, and I like accidentally found her behind this tree. So we took off and decided to find her uncle. Which is where we were going when she fell in the mud. And then you showed up. Where's dessert?"

"And where is Grace's uncle?" asked Lady Lira.

"Other side of the South Queen—we think." He looked to Grace for corroboration. She was propped on her elbows and breathing rhythmically.

"How did you know that?" asked Lady Lira. Then she seemed to catch herself. "Perhaps we should let the young lady retire and save the dessert for tomorrow. The chocolate will easily keep."

"Oh, no," said Lance in a panic. "I can tell you. It's this guy she met at the trailhead. He's the one that said the road was gone. He said he went climbing with Grace's uncle and was gonna pick him up on the other side of the mountain. He had a poem that her uncle wrote. She recognized the writing."

"How lovely," said Lady Lira. "I'm so fond of poetry. What was the poem about?"

"Beats me," said Lance. "She never said." He looked over his shoulder at the wooden door whence dinner had emerged on the pitter-patter of furry feet.

Lady Lira scrutinized Grace, who was slumbering sweetly, her face in her palms. Then the woman leaned across the table toward Lance. Her long dark hair brushed over her shoulders; her low-cut gown revealed uncharted territories. "Perhaps," she said softly, "someone as clever as—"

But here Grace's elbows caved in. She crashed to her plate, and the whole table rattled. Grace looked up in stupid wonder. Her cheeks were dripping with grease. What place was this? What companions were these? She saw a fleshy boy whose eyes burned with longing. She saw a dark woman whose eyes burned with knowledge. She saw a stone-faced rodent whose eyes had burned to ashes. The eyes were upon her in a large, dark cavern. And she feared them all.

10

She awoke in a sea of soft green light. It was morning, and Grace was still in the house of Lady Lira. Her shoulders ached as she turned. At home, turning in bed set off undulating tides that rocked her back to sleep. But this bed was firm, like a beach. She was not at home.

Beyond the window were many fir trees, row on row, festooned with chartreuse lichen. The trees kept the shores of the mossy bog. Nearer at hand, the window ledge outside the glass bore ranks of fruiting cups. They stood on end like pale green trumpets waiting to sound the judgment. She put her nose on a single pane and, straining her eyes, could barely glimpse the landing below. Alongside it, the barge was waiting. Eight small marmots were slumped in the traces.

Grace turned over once again and looked about the bedroom. There was a stone fireplace, two straight chairs, a green hearth rug. This rug too had a swollen red dragon in the center. Grace studied its fatness with special disinterest and closed her eyes to sleep.

Then without warning, the door to the bedroom opened wide, and in came Lance, still wearing the billowy shirt that Lady Lira had given him. Apparently, it had not occurred to him to knock.

"Breakfast is over," he announced. "Thought I'd tell ya."

He looked at the dragon. He looked at the fireplace. He did not look at Grace.

Grace, meanwhile, had pulled the covers tight to her lips. "Okay by me," she said. "Not hungry."

"The bacon, I tell ya—fantastic bacon."

"Mm," said Grace, and planted a rancid pause.

Lance looked past her out the window. "Awesome place, huh?"

"Awesome," she echoed.

"Be kinda fun to stay here a while, no?"

"No doubt," said she.

"Lady Lira says if I want, I can go with her and catch marmots today. She trains them and everything."

"Amazing," said Grace.

"Sounds pretty great if you ask me, hunting marmots."

"A fine time, indeed," she answered.

Lance sensed something amiss. "Grace," he requested, "will you shove it?"

"Sorry, Lance. I'm not the pushy type."

"Don't you like it here?" he demanded. "She seems a little strange, yeah, but once you get to know her—"

"Like you have?"

"Well, yeah—sort of. We had a nice talk at breakfast, anyway." He paused. "Listen. She says it's impossible to find your uncle. Too dangerous. If you go over the pass like we wanted to, you hit these big mother glaciers with humungous cracks in the ice. You slip right in and nobody ever finds you. And if you go around the mountain instead, you hit these river gorges with no bridges or nothing. Too deep to cross. You drown for sure if you try. Lady Lira says we can stay here a few days, and then she'll take us out to the road when she's got time. Sounds like a plan, doesn't it?"

"A most sensible plan, Lance."

"You serious?"

She thought it over. She was none too good at walking on bogs. They would leave as they had come—in Lady Lira's barge and at Lady Lira's pleasure.

"Serious," she said.

"Good," he replied. "Glad you agree."

He looked to the floor in a way that imported a weighty transition. "Besides," he added, "are you for sure positive it was your uncle's writing you saw? People's handwriting can look real similar, you know."

"True," said Grace.

"So it might not have been his."

"Possibly not," she said.

"What did it say, anyway? You never told me. I guess I'm sorta curious."

"The poem?" she asked

"Yeah, what's in it?"

She drew a deep breath and knotted her forehead as if making up her mind. Then she exhaled with considerable calm. "Sorry if I forgot to let you in on it," she said. "Because you do deserve to know. Here, I'll get you some paper and something to write with—and you can copy it down if you want. I just have it in my head." She drew pen and notebook from the pack by her bed and tore out a sheet for him. "Okay. Pull up a chair. Ready?"

"Ready," said Lance.

Grace sat up straight and cleared her throat. "Listen carefully. All right? Here goes:

> "*'Twas brillig, and—*"

"'Twas what?"

"*Brillig*. You know—one of those Old-English-type words for 'stormy.' Shakespeare uses it all the time."

"Mm," he said. He got it partway written before the pen punched through the paper in his lap.

> *"'Twas brillig, and the slithy toves—"*

"Wait a minute. *Toves*?"
"Right. They're a really yummy sort of mushroom."
"How do you spell it?"
"Just like it sounds: T-O-A-F-Z."
Lance labored the letters into print.

> *"'Twas brillig, and the slithy toves—"*

"I thought you said *slimy* toafz."
"No, no, no. *Slithy*. Where do you go to school, anyway?"
He lit up. "West Central. Undefeated the last two years in—"
"Here," cut in Grace. "You just listen, and I'll write it down for you when I finish."
He gladly surrendered the paper and pen.

> *"'Twas brillig, and the slithy toves*
> *Did gyre and gimble in the wabe:*
> *All mimsy were the borogoves,*
> *And the mome raths outgrabe."*

"The what-raths?" he asked.
"I'll write it down for you," she said.

> *"Beware the Jabberwock, my son!*
> *The jaws that bite, the claws that catch!*
> *Beware the Jubjub bird, and shun*
> *The frumious Bandersnatch!*
>
> *He took his vorpal sword in hand:*
> *Long time the manxome foe he sought—"*

At this point memory failed. Grace broke off.

"Is that all?" said Lance. "Sounds to me like it's just getting started."

"No, that's the end," she insisted. "It's sort of an *avant garde* poem. You're not supposed to live happily ever after."

"Oh," said Lance. He wondered if an *avant garde* were anything like a Jubjub bird. He got up from the chair and paced the rug while Grace wrote out the poem. She gave it to him, and he shoved it in his voluminous shirt.

"Sure you don't want to go marmot hunting?" he asked.

"I never said I didn't," said Grace. "But now that you mention it, I'm sure that I don't."

"See ya then. Gotta go. Leaving pretty soon. Back tonight, I guess." He said all this from the door.

"While you're out in the woods," said Grace, "pick me some toves for supper, will you?"

"Sure," said Lance. "I bet there's lots of 'em."

"Thanks," said Grace. "Thanks a lot."

"That's my name," he smiled.

"What's your name?"

"Lott."

"Sure. Thanks a lot, Lancelot."

"Not Lance E. Lott. Lance Q. Lott."

"Q? As in Quincy? Quentin? Quizzler? Queer?"

Lance bristled, then reddened. "Quercus," he said.

Grace rolled her eyes.

When Lance was gone, Grace paged to the real poem in her notebook.

> *A gentle wight for gentle ladies three*
> *Aduentured through a verdant wood newgrowne,*
> *Through wildernesse that mote a wastlond bee,*
> *Vnless he greete the greenwood for his owne,*
> *Vnless he know the leaf as ice and stone.*

Faine needs he find a maid of faerie eyne,
To spie the shielde vpon the second throne,
To limn therein the ledgers ancient line—
Lest Beast and woman darke the northerne morning
  shyne.

She pondered the words—but not for long, for the door swung open once more. Anyone entering could have seen her cram the notebook in her pack—anyone, that is, save a marmot balancing a tray of toast and eggs and tea and bacon on his head—which is who it was. She looked at him with amused relief. Was it "her" marmot? She thought so—he seemed younger than James and smaller than the marmots in the traces outside. Now he walked precariously across the floor and slid the tray on her bed.

"You're so cute!" she gushed. "I can't stand it."

He toppled backwards as if overcome by the compliment. Grace laughed until her bed shook half the tea from its cup. The marmot took his cue. He sulked to the door, tail dragging.

"Wait," she called. "Come back, slithy marmot."

He looked at her in a mimsy way.

"Come here. I want to pet you."

The marmot considered for a marmot moment. Then he nosed his way back and lithely sprang to the foot of the bed. Grace leaned forward and very gently touched his wet nose. He quivered but did not move away.

"You're a good fellow," she told him. "Remember that."

She sat back and ate her breakfast and watched her marmot. Unlike any dog or cat she had known, he did not come snooping across the covers to sniff at her food. After a while he did not even watch her plate—instead he gazed out the window. Grace mopped up the last bit of eggs and looked out too. She saw what he saw: Lady Lira, James, and Lance gliding away on the marmot-drawn sled. It made silent sweeping turns around clumps of devil's club.

"Do you wish you were going too?" she asked the marmot. He looked at her blankly. From out the window she thought she heard—she might have heard—the faintest snap of a whip.

Breakfast done, she helped the marmot carry the dishes down the stairs and across the hall, now faintly sunlit and very dusty and not nearly as foreboding as the night before. When they got to the table, two marmots pattered from the door on the right and took their dishes. Then they were left in the dim hall alone—no place, Grace decided, to spend the day. She recrossed the carpet to the entryway. The marmot followed after.

The door was unlocked, but she needed her shoulder to shove it open—it was that heavy. Outside, her feet slapped cool on the stone landing. The air was fresh but mosquito-laden, humming like a pitch pipe blown in anger. On the mossy cliff above she could see the niche of her bedroom window. At the top of the cliff poised a patch of blue sky far away.

She sat down on the edge of the landing and watched a mosquito drill her knee. She let it drink deep and fly away, let the white welt burn and rise in her skin. The others she would kill. Her toes fell to dabbling on the surface of the bog. It shook like gelatin, rippled like a waterbed. In time the marmot crept beside her and let her stroke his neck. His hair was full and coarse. While her one hand nurtured, the other dealt doom, and a score of mosquitoes breathed their last in swift and bloody explosions.

"It's going to be a long day," she sighed.

Heeding the prophecy, the marmot circled behind her back and curled up to sleep. She too lay back, pillowed her head on the obliging marmot and shut her eyes. For a while her hands reflexively swatted all comers. But soon they lay at peace in her lap, and her feet sank quietly through the moss and disappeared in ooze.

And so she slept, and the day wore on, and mosquitoes fed in armies on her flesh. When at last she awoke, the sun flamed red in the trees. It felt late. Her face was swollen, her back was aching, her feet were frigid. The patient marmot had not moved; he still lay under her head.

Grace sat up and shivered. "Wake up," she told the marmot. He uncurled himself and stretched like a cat. Grace sucked her feet from out of the bog, got up, staggered to the door, and pried it open with both heels planted. The marmot slipped in. After wiping the mud from her feet, she followed.

The great hall was silent and chilly—no one had started a fire. From a few high windows, dusty red sunbeams angled to the carpet. One burned the dragon in the center.

Grace shivered again and ran upstairs for her down jacket. The bedroom was eerie. Instead of the soft green light of morning, an orange glare filled the chamber. Grace plucked the jacket from her pack. On impulse, she snatched her notebook too. She tore out the poem, put it in her pocket, and then fled downstairs to the marmot.

Together they sat at the empty table. The jacket helped, but her feet were still cold. She tried to slip them under the marmot; the marmot sidled away. So, naturally, she thought of the shoes Lady Lira had promised. Had the woman forgotten? She looked at the door on the left of the fireplace. It was only a few steps away. Perhaps Lady Lira would not mind. It would take but a minute to find a pair—just an *old* pair. But then—was she the type to go picking through someone else's wardrobe? She was not. Lady Lira should soon be home. She could wait that long.

Grace tucked her feet beneath her knees, Indian fashion, and patiently sat for as long as anyone reasonably could. But her feet got no warmer, and in three minutes, perhaps, the door got the best of her. She arose and stole past the hearth on tiptoe, making no sound. But she was not brave enough. An accomplice was needed. "Come on," she whispered, and the marmot obligingly padded behind her.

Grace pushed open the wooden door and peered inside. She saw a modest-sized room, candle-lit but deserted. Shadows flickered on the ropy lava ceiling. She slipped in and held the door open for the marmot. He hesitated on the threshold, his silver fur quaking. "We're just going to find a couple shoes, that's all," said Grace. The marmot entered, froze, then shot beneath a four-poster bed that filled one side of the room.

"What a chicken," she murmured, and let the door close. She saw a red dragon on the green bed quilt, another on a carpet at her feet. An oval table with two chairs stood opposite the bed. It held two smoothly burning candles and a very large letter opener. She saw neither closets nor bureaus nor any stray shoes. (This was not like Grace's room at home, where shoes were scattered like mushrooms in a forest.) But the corners of the chamber were very dark. Perhaps there was a wardrobe in the shadows by the bed.

She stepped towards the darkness. The silence was stifling. She wanted to tell the marmot to come out from hiding. But she didn't tell him anything.

There! Something moved. It was across the bed at eye level. Grace stood very still and looked at the shadows. Whatever it was had stopped. Then she saw them—two bright eyes, marking her intently. She met the gaze and glimpsed and guessed the outline of a face. She could not bear it long. She opened her mouth to speak, perchance to scream—and so did the other.

And then she knew. "It's just a mirror!" laughed Grace, her fears relieved. Her reflection laughed nervously with her.

Grace made her way around the bed and stood before a

full-length glass in the shadows. "I look awful," she whispered. Her long brown hair was tangled. Her nose was sunburnt and peeling. Her face and arms and legs were bruised and scratched and mosquito-ravaged. She had never looked like this before. Quietly she gazed, mentally repairing her image.

Then she saw something more. The corner of the mirror reflected two pinpoints of candlelight. They had softly burned there all along. Now, however, they blazed more intently. She was sure of it. She looked behind her at the candles on the table. They burned as smoothly as before. She looked again at the tapers in the mirror. They were two eyes now, glowing in darkness, hovering at the shoulder of her double in the glass. She wheeled around—there was no one in the room. Then she faced the mirror again. The two eyes were there still, resolute, and brighter if anything. Now, around them, was it?—a face was gathering substance there. A moan escaped her. It was a man's face, an old man's face, an old man's face with a wealth of white hair and an aged beard.

"Uncle Garth?" she whispered.

A hand in the mirror touched her shoulder, or its reflection, anyway. Did she not feel it? The man in the mirror called to her as if she were far away. "Grace," he said. She was glad and ashamed to hear him call her name. "Come," he told her, and the hand in the mirror tugged gently on her shoulder as if trying to turn her around.

Her reflection did not budge. She wanted to ask her uncle where he was and where she was and how she could find him. This she was about to do when she heard a voice at the door.

"James! This way."

Uncle Garth faded like morning mist. For one terrible moment, Grace stood before the mirror and watched only her eyes, transfixed by her widening pupils. Then two furry paws grasped her ankles, and she dropped to the floor and slipped under the bed. As she did so, Lady Lira entered the room.

"James!"

Grace's breath revolved in shallow pats. Her marmot quivered beneath her arm. His whiskers tickled her nose. She would sneeze, she knew it.

"James!"

The voice was next to the table now. Lady Lira seemed impatient. Two pair of paws came through the door. Grace could just see them through the fringe of the quilt.

"What?" said a voice. Apparently, the marmot himself had spoken. Grace was too frightened to wonder at it.

"Sit down, James."

"What?" James must have been somewhat deaf, for Grace could hear Lady Lira quite clearly.

"Sit down, worthless marmot, and hear better. Your hide will make a tender morsel yet."

"No—I mean yes," he said briskly.

Grace heard two chairs scuff the carpet. She felt bacon rising in her gorge. It was stuffy under the bed.

"He didn't have the nerve," hissed Lady Lira. "The sentimental ass. He's giving it up—letting someone else do his dirty work. Well, it has taken him years enough to make up his mind. You, James—"

"What?"

"You—just a puppy when he first had the chance. How long I have waited! And now his chance is squandered. The fool! He thinks the ax can pass to another beneath my very nose—and I not find it first? Hah! Once cast away, it belongs to whoever can snatch it. And if I can't, James, if I can't, I'll snatch the ones it's meant for.

"And such weaklings! It was always his way. I could hardly fear them even with the ax in their hands. It's almost an insult—sending filthy little children to spy on my doorstep. I nearly had them murdered in their beds last night—a pity I needed to find out more. As it is, the young prince of the feast has used up his tenure. Poem indeed! I doubt the ax is meant for that clodpoll. Even so, it was wise of you to suggest we put him out of the way, James. I am glad we have done it."

"Thank you," said James.

"Now, the girl," said Lady Lira.

To Grace it sounded as if the woman had turned to face the bed.

"A most wary, spiteful creature. Blood kin to him—I knew it from the moment I first saw her eyes. She may not know what she is about, but she will help him just the same. That's his way—very unfair, too. She knows enough to fear me, though, and that's too much.

"Where is the little bitch? Sleeping, no doubt, if she drank the drowsy potion in her tea. Check her room, James."

"What?"

"Check her room, I say—and her pack too. Take anything that's written. And when you find her, bring her downstairs to the fire," she added. "Perhaps we can find ways—wonderful ways—to prompt a poetry recital."

Lady Lira began a drawn-out laugh, and James started padding to the door.

"We have her sure," the woman cackled. "There's no way out save through the looking glass, and she'll need more than fairy blood to discover that."

James left, and Lady Lira's feet approached the bed. Her slippered heels stepped around to the mirror and came to rest just inches from where Grace lay hidden. She could easily have bitten them and almost wanted to. Part of her was calm enough to wonder if the woman saw anything more than her own reflection in the mirror. There was no way of knowing.

Then Lady Lira began to speak. No, she was not speaking, really, but chanting in a solemn voice:

You will be fed,
You must be fed,
You shall be fed.
Devour, devour, devour this day
Your daily bread.
Devour this day your daily bread.

Grace nearly vomited. The marmot beneath her arm grew stiff as stone. Lady Lira repeated the chant in deadly earnest:

You will be fed,
You must be fed,
You shall be fed.
Devour, devour, devour this day
Your daily bread.
Devour this day your daily bread.

It sounded nothing like her and everything like her. She went on, turning and returning the words, gathering intensity of pledge and prayer and promise. It seemed to Grace that the mirror must shatter.

But then, as abruptly as she had begun, Lady Lira broke off and paced away. The door opened and closed as she quit the room.

Grace lay more still than ever. She thought of her future. Any minute now, Lady Lira would find she was not upstairs. Then they would check on the front landing. Then they would check in the kitchen. Then they would check here. Beyond that, she refused to think.

Her hand crept from beneath the bed and grasped the bottom corner of the mirror. She pulled gently, and the mirror swung open like the front of a medicine cabinet. Out poked her head, in she looked. A single candle burned beside a bath. Steaming water purled over the lip, just as it did upstairs. Beyond the bath was an open wardrobe. Gowns of all colors were waiting in glory and rows of shoes beneath them. Next to the wardrobe was another door.

Grace smothered the marmot to her breast and crawled behind the mirror. Then she pulled it shut behind her—it closed without a click. She stood up, trembling. The door beside the wardrobe beckoned. She crossed the room, turned the knob—and stood on the threshold of darkness. It seemed to be a tunnel, a passage. There was no telling where it might lead. There was no time to guess.

She grabbed the burning candle and stepped inside. Her feet came down on tiny things unutterably sharp. She jumped back. The candlelight showed spikes of lava, crowding the floor of the passage. It was time to get the shoes she had come for. She turned to the wardrobe and chose what looked sturdy—a tough leather pair, boots really, with thongs that wrapped to the knee. She fumbled with the thongs while the marmot looked on. "Don't wait for me," she whispered. But he did anyway. When her shoes were fastened, she ushered him on ahead through the door. It closed behind them soundlessly.

Once in the tunnel, Grace discovered that even with her leather boots the lava spikes were sharp. She walked as if she were plagued with blisters, holding the candle unsteadily aloft. The marmot, though, had no such problem. He romped as if through grassy meadows, staying just at the edge of the candle's pooled light.

For many steps the way continued straight and level. Then it split in two. One fork led onward, the other up and left. The marmot stopped, stood up on his hind legs, sniffed the air. Then he burrowed up the left-hand passage, and Grace followed. The new way angled steeply upward and kept on bending left. Grace clutched at the wall to balance her steps. The going was even slower.

At any moment she expected to hear the echo behind her

of a door unlatching and Lady Lira's "There they are!" that would unleash a horde of marmots, eager to devour their daily bread. But instead, after many steps, she felt a hint of a breeze in her face; the candle began to sputter.

"I think we're almost out," she whispered. And then they were out, for needles and branches were scratching her face, and through them she saw the twilight sky. She ducked low to get through, and something met her elbow. She thought it was the marmot at first. But it was not the marmot. Whatever it was was leaning against the entrance of the cave. She needed several moments to see what it used to be. For the pack was partly burnt, partly shredded in strips that hung from the metal frame. She quickly stepped back; her feet touched a soft lumpish shape on the floor. Her hand jumped, and the candle flame erased itself in the breeze. In spite of herself, she bent down and groped in the dark — more tattered nylon, caked with something. And then she felt the limp grasp of a mitten.

"Eeow!" she screamed.

In that same instant a glow appeared far down the tunnel, and with the glow came the echo of a cry: "After her!"

Grace and her marmot burst through the branches like wood grouse flushed from cover. The stars arose to the very occasion, and girl and marmot wildly ran in their broken beams, through stones, through grass, through dewy night.

11

HER VOICE AWAKENED HIM. "You're not so hurt as I'd thought," she said.

I'm not? he wondered. William lay stiffly on a sweet-smelling pallet of grass. Above him he saw wooden beams, around him walls of stone. The woman was rubbing his hair-less chest with something moist and cool. William lifted his head and caught sight of himself. He gawked. His chest was raked in a musical score of scabby lines. He raised his shoul-ders, but this hurt him sorely. So he let the woman push him back. Now he recalled it: a roar in the night, a blast of breath, a slicing of flesh—and now the coolness and a woman's hands.

"Must've been a bear," he mumbled.

"A bear," she said, considering. Through a window came the doubting notes of a mountain chickadee—one high, two low, in a minor key, the unsure announcement of morning come. Pieces of sunshine came in at a door and roamed the woman's hair. It was brown, like her smock. Her eyes were very green, and her nose was splendidly sunburnt.

"Here," she said. "Now that you've awakened, I will answer your questions."

"But I haven't asked any," William shot back.

"All the more reason to have them," she replied.

Why was he so obstinate? That was one question, anyway.

"First," she said, "my name is Lady Demaris."

"*Lady* Demaris?" he queried. "Not Ms.?"

"Ms." She tasted the word. For a moment her fingers lay still on his chest. "No, I should think I am Lady Demaris."

"I'm William," he volunteered.

"Thank you," she told him. "Last night, William, my herdsman found you in a cave about three miles off. He heard you shouting and discovered you alone—a bit mauled, as you see. Luckily, it was only toying with you."

"The bear?" he asked

She was silent for a moment. "It was not a bear," she said quietly. "You might as well know. You were found at the door of the Lava Beast."

The Lava Beast. The words burned his chest and darkened his mind. William had never heard the name, but he felt inexplicably that he knew the creature. "I see," he said, and nodded.

"You are fortunate," she continued. "A little deeper, and he would have torn your heart." She began to knead his sternum softly. William could feel his intact ventricles flutter against her fingertips.

It dawned on him what he ought to say. "I must thank you," he told her. Then he added, "What's the ointment you've got there?"

"Something," she said, "to make you whole. But this afternoon, when you are ready, find Colin outside. He is the one to thank."

He grunted, the way he did to reward a woman for a job well done. Then he lay silent and relished the cool massage. At the other end of the room he could see a sleeping loft. Underneath was a rough wooden table with stools. On the wall nearby hung cups, pots, and a large wooden pail. The pail was by the door that was letting in the sun.

"You live up here, Lady Demaris?"

103

"This is my home, yes."

"Year round? Even in winter?"

"Even in winter."

"Amazing," he said. "So what do you do?"

"I care for the place."

"This cabin? That doesn't take much, does it?"

"No," she said. "But I mean the whole place." She took one hand from off his chest and waved it toward the door.

"So you own a few acres up here—a little inholding?"

"I own none of it. All that lies beneath the Queens, I care for."

"But this is wilderness," said William. "No one needs to take care of it. You just leave it alone. That's what makes it wilderness."

"Ah," she said, "but that's the problem." Her voice and her green eyes dropped. "There are those who will not leave it alone."

Her answer made him cross. "Lady Demaris," he said, "do you think there is such a thing as too much wilderness?"

She made no reply.

"I mean," he continued, "lately I've seen more trees than I ever cared to."

She removed her hands, and his wounds stung deep. Her eyes met his in a pitying way, and he shrank beneath the load of condescension that he felt. He much preferred Rational Discussion to Knowing Looks.

But he backed down a little. "So tell me, what are you doing these days—'to care for the place'?"

"Right now," she said, "it's the marmots."

"The marmots," he repeated sagely.

"Yes. They normally go where they will, but lately they've been preyed upon. You see, Lady Lira, my sister—" Here she broke off and bit her lip. "My sister seizes them almost daily. Some she trains for her service. A few she completely corrupts to her will. But most of them she feeds—to the Lava Beast himself."

William felt again the dark hush of the name.

"Once we cared for the forests together, but now she serves—him. It is very sad to me. Perhaps you cannot understand it all."

William attempted a skeptical nod, but it came off with reverence.

"Colin and I watch the marmots in the meadows now to keep them from my sister. We are never completely successful—there are just the two of us. I imagine the Lava Beast did not eat you because he had devoured his fill for the day. Whatever we can save from Lady Lira and the Lava Beast we do—that is part of why Colin saved you. Perhaps right now—in caring for you, William—I am caring for this place. I do not know. It may happen you will be of great help someday."

This was unsettling. William did not like the way she had slipped in his first name. But he decided to humor her. Or was he curious?

"Why does the Lava Beast need your sister?" he asked. "Can't he catch his own marmots?"

"The Lava Beast," said Lady Demaris, "is a creature of darkness. Even the pure cold starlight of winter is noxious to him. He never ventures from his caves, and no marmot is foolish enough to venture in. So he relies on his devoted ones to appease his appetite."

"What does he look like?" asked William.

"Some say—" she began, but then she halted. "I do not know. I've never seen him."

William pounced on the admission. "Then how can you be sure there *is* a Lava Beast?"

She touched his raw and scabby stripes. "By his deeds," she said. "Though seldom seen, he makes his mark—in all of us, I'm afraid. He is too often near, and when we doubt his presence, then he is closest."

William felt dishonest for having asked. Somehow he was sure of the Lava Beast himself. "So why does your sister work for him?"

"That is a mystery to me. Perhaps it is the lava mansion he gave her. But it's such a dark, hollow place—I don't understand why she wanted it. Perhaps it is the clothes he gave her and the servants. I do not know. Her gowns are splendid now, but her skin is pale as death. And the servants—I can't tell why she needs them. Maybe she tired of bringing the water up from the stream to our cottage."

Here she looked at the wooden pail hung up by the door. She put her hands in her lap and sat very still. "But she doesn't just 'work for him,' as you say. She is part of him now. It is as if he has eaten her too."

"So why don't you stop her?" he asked.

"It is not that easily done. She will not listen to me now—I have little power against her. She's very strong, and she has many marmots to enforce her will. And even if I were able, I know I could not harm her. She is still my sister.

"But there is a weapon by which the servants of the Lava Beast are felled. Some say it will wound the head of the Lava Beast himself. Once, I think, it was a great sword, and before that, a rod in the desert. But now it is an ice ax."

William narrowed his eyes.

"The ax belongs to an old man now. He often walks this way. Other servants of the Beast he has felled in his time, but now he is loath to wield the ax."

"Too old?" said William.

"No, he is not feeble. It is just that—" She stopped for a moment. Her green eyes glistened. "You see—he loved my sister. Before she chose the Lava Beast, she was nearly wedded to Garth. It is hard to believe now. Morning by morning they strolled in the meadows hand in hand. He made songs for her, put lupines in her hair, found for her the first wild strawberries. On summer eves they raced to the golden snows of the Center Queen. There they slid down reckless slopes, clasped together, shadowed in spray, shouting aloft to the first-formed stars. No one knew two better lovers.

"Then on the midsummer morning of their wedding day, Garth came to the cottage to wake his bride. The sun had cleared the Center Queen; the meadow shone with dew. Behind him tumbled troops of marmots, all wearing garlands of bluebells and buttercups. Colin came romping and singing among them, and all the marmots were whistling in time. Ah, I remember they made such joy! 'Come out!' they sang. 'Come out, sweet Lira! Today you'll be married, be married today!' I opened wide the door to them and led Garth to the loft to wake his bride."

Lady Demaris and William looked up at the loft.

"And it was empty. Sometime before dawn she had slipped away. And I, up early gathering herbs and flowers, had not seen."

Lady Demaris shook her head. "No, he will not use the ax anymore. It is time—past time he surrendered it to another."

This brought on a thoughtful silence. She gazed at William in a way that guessed possibilities.

"Don't look at me," he croaked.

Lady Demaris stood up and smiled, still gazing at him. For a moment her hair shone bravely in the sunlight from the doorway. Then she turned, slipped the wooden bucket off the wall, and vanished outside.

William gazed after her. He had seen it in her eyes. She thought him heir apparent to the tool and trade of a vicious assassin. He would tell her nothing—not a thing, to strengthen his claim to that inheritance. He lay his head back on the sweet-smelling grass. His eyes wandered over the rafters. Nothing. He would say nothing. He was sure. He kept repeating it, rafter by rafter. Nothing. Nothing. Then he slept.

When William awoke, the room was still and noonlike. He heard no birds. One fly buzzed his head like a chain saw. He sat up slowly, expecting very great pain in his chest—but it barely ached. His wounds, in fact, were whitening into scars. He touched them. Where was their sting?

Lady Demaris appeared in the doorway. "How do you feel?" she asked.

"Tell me," said William, "what's in the ointment?"

"Oh. Many good things," she laughed. "But how are you feeling?"

"Like what things?"

She whimsically tilted her head in the air. "Let's see. North-facing moss from a thousand-year cedar, timberline dew from a midsummer morning, stamens of arnica, gloss from a buttercup, hoarfrost and ice worms and snow watermelons. Tender tips of staghorn lichen, buckwheat pollen, sap from a whitebark, fiddlehead hearts that are cut in the moonlight—and one lavender shooting star. It has to be northward pointing, too, and that sort is hard to come by." She smiled, obviously proud of her recipe.

William shook his head.

"There's lunch on the step," she said, pointing behind her, "if you feel up to it."

William shambled to the door and sat down on the step. He found a loaf of hot bread and a pitcher of water—also a salad of much that was green but nothing that was lettuce. He ate it anyway. He was no vegetarian (more a chocolaterian), but it went down well. He turned to Lady Demaris in the cottage behind him: "What's in the salad?"

She slyly tilted her head again.

"Never mind," said William quickly.

The sun shone squarely on his white and hairless chest. It

was a good feeling, a new feeling. He wondered why he had always hid in polypropylene. He drank huge gulps of water, and some of it dripped from his chin to his belly. There was a slight breeze, and it cooled his wet flesh wonderfully.

He looked out from the step to a brook that splashed down a grassy ravine and entered the forest below. Above, it gushed from glaciers that tongued their way from the Center Queen to the meadows. He lifted his eyes to the mountain. It was perfect in symmetry—one vast shimmering dome. The ice shone white, silvery white in the noonday sun. To the left, behind a grove in the meadows, he saw the North Queen too. Like the South, it rose in lava cliffs, crossed by amber and burgundy bands. Unlike the South Queen, its summit mounted above the cliffs to a snowy crater ring. This made the North Queen highest of all.

His lunch finished, William rose to wander down the brook. He wore no boots, and his toes sank softly in the grass. This was new. Down by the water the lupine grew thick and covered his feet completely. The hot sun probed his shoulders now, and so did the mosquitoes. Should he return for a shirt? Or shoes? His feet voted otherwise. Damn the mosquitoes— half speed ahead! So on he sauntered through bits of meadow and streamside gardens and groves of fir and hemlock. He felt brave and soft and careless. He had never walked in alpine parkland just to walk. Always he had been madly en route to a summit or a car. He was somewhere he had never been.

By and by, along the stream he came upon a field of marmots snuffling in the flowers. He walked in among them, and none seemed to care. The marmots neither ran nor piped nor even looked at him. Across their pasture under a stand of mountain hemlock, a young man lay on his side in the shade. The youth was singing softly, and William drew near to listen. This much he heard:

"Beneath a forest shade I watch
My marmots feed beneath the sun;
Upon the dawn they come to me
And go when day is done.
When day is done, I lay me down to sleep,
And Rosamond my thoughts like marmots keep.

"Beneath a forest shade I hear
The brook new-shed from mountain snows;
In morning it runs shallowly,
At noon it overflows.
At noon I lay me down beside the stream,
And Rosamond then overflows my dream.

"Beneath a forest shade I touch
The lupine one and two and ten;
The sunrise brings new drops of dew,
And sunset brings again.
The sunset brings to me the parting hour,
When lupine fade, but Rosamond may flower."

The young man sighed and dug his toes in the grass. Then he turned on his back and looked upwards through the branches. William stood by, too far away to introduce himself and too close to blend with the scenery. He could not tell whether the young man saw him.

Finally he called out in a yoo-hoo sort of voice, "Hello! Are you Colin?"

"I am," said the youth, still contemplating the branches. "And you, old man—how are you feeling?"

"Very well," said William, "thanks to you, I think."

Colin abandoned his arboreal vision. He leapt to his feet, ran to William, slapped him on the back. "Glad to hear it!" he told him. He inspected William's scars with approval and then invited him into the shade. "It's a little hot just now," he said.

They sat down together. It was cool in the shade, and William sprouted a crop of goose bumps. Colin put his hand on William's knee. "On a day like today," he confided, "'tis right for a contest."

"A contest?" said William.

"A singing match," said Colin.

"I don't sing so well," William said. "I can't even read music."

"I don't read music either," said Colin. "I sing it. You must try—the time and the place require you."

"Require me?" said William.

"First we must think what to sing of. Ah! It is clear. I shall sing of Rosamond, and you of your own love. Line for line, thus: I sing one line, and you answer with your own."

William looked reluctant.

"What's the matter?" asked Colin. "Have you no lady love?"

"Well, no. I'm too busy with computers."

"Aha! The lovely Computressa—you cannot keep her name from your lips."

"No! Not her. I mean, not them."

"There is no lady in your life then? None whom you seek? None?"

"Not really. Except, well, right now I'm looking for a girl named Grace. Have you seen her?"

"No. Sing of her heavenly beauty, though, and she will grow nearer to your heart. But lovely as she is, she cannot compare to my Rosamond—the nonpareil, the inexpressive she."

"But—"

"Say no more," Colin assured him. "I know your concerns. We have need of referees for our contest. Luckily they are close at hand. Marmots have a very fine ear for music. Ho! Over here, you rascals! You must judge our singing match!"

Ten of the closest marmots galloped to the shade and stood in a line, testing the air with their whiskers. "Ready?" said Colin. They all looked it. So he began to sing:

"I saw a fair young mountain maid
Holay, holay, holay-o . . ."

He paused, and the jury of marmots turned their heads toward William, who sang nothing.

"Here," said Colin gallantly, "I'll assist you. Now you must sing something like this.

"A-walking in the forest glade
Upon the first of May-o.

"See? That's not so hard."

William started to shiver. The shade was green ice. Colin began again:

"Her hair it shone the finest gold
Amidst the morning ray-o."

The marmots looked at William.

"What?" said Colin. "Still stumped, my friend? Think what you wish to praise about your Grace. What is it that delights you most? What of her lovely hair?"

"Her hair?" said William. "I've never seen it combed. It was dirty."

"Her eyes, then," said Colin.

"Her eyes," echoed William. "Her eyes have a certain—it's hard to . . . Wait a minute, what have you got me—"

Just here William was cut short. Urgent whistling shot from afar. At once their jury joined the call and blasted in a chorus. Colin jumped to his feet. "Trouble," he said. He grabbed his staff and sped barefoot across the grass into a grove of trees.

This left William alone in a sea of piping marmots. He stumbled out into the sun and looked on every side. Go! said the whistling marmots. Go somewhere! Knowing no better direction, William ran where Colin had. But halfway to the grove of trees he stepped in a hole and landed flat on his hairless chest—so flat that he lost his wind. Facedown in the lupine, biting the earth, he manfully fought to breathe.

The whistling redoubled behind him. At first, paralyzed as he was, he could not look. Then he turned his green-stained face—and marveled. The jury of marmots he'd left behind were bundled in a net, bumping in tow behind the strides of a woman dressed in green. A silvery marmot trotted at her side. She had to be the sister, strange and estranged, of Lady Demaris.

William rose and shouted at her: "What are you doing! Hey! Hey!" He wanted to thunder an ultimatum, but he could not find the words. His voice was quivering badly.

The woman turned her head and laughed at him. Her eyes pierced his, and he shivered in their shade. Then she spoke something to the marmot beside her and strode on.

Immediately the marmot rushed him. It glowered and hissed and bared its teeth. William froze, then sprinted in terror. If a peaceable marmot could slash one's heel, what could a rampaging marmot inflict? It was wonderful how William sped. He leapt, he ran, he flew half-crazed. He stepped in no holes and tripped on no logs. It was terrible how William felt. He sweat, he bled, he panted, he foamed. He crashed through trees and coated himself with twigs and needles and cones and lichen. Finally, his lungs afire, he came upon Colin in a faraway clearing and collapsed at his feet, groveling in asthmatic frenzy.

"Don't let him—" he gasped. "A ferocious, the most ferocious, you ever saw."

Colin looked puzzled. "You must have outrun him, old man."

William looked fearfully behind. The groves and the grass were at peace.

"I think I know the one you mean," said Colin. "A big hoary fellow that she keeps with her. Did you see the woman too?"

William nodded. "A netful," he panted. "She took a whole netful. Tried to stop her. Sorry."

"Blast her name!" cried Colin. "I've been decoyed! All that was here was a young boy tangled in his net." He pointed to the net lying empty on the grass. "I made *him* black and blue for his trouble—before he ran off. But what's the good?"

"I tried," said William meekly.

"No, not your fault, man. She does have a fierce marmot or two. Nothing you could do without a staff of your own."

This made William feel better.

"Beastly business," Colin muttered.

In the evening the marmots dispersed to their burrows. William and Colin walked upstream, and the dew brushed cool on their feet. The creek was full, the mosquitoes at rest. A chickadee called that day was done, and then proved it so with silence. At a bend in the stream they saw the cottage. Its windows were faintly lit. Above, out of the darkening meadows, the Center Queen rose all tinted with pink.

William let Colin go ahead. He stood very still in a cloak that he had borrowed from Colin and rested his eyes on the peak in the alpenglow. There were no Good Routes there, nothing to interest a Serious Climber—only solace for a serious mind. His gaze descended to the dampening meadows, and then to the curtained hemlocks at his side. The trees and the grass were pleasant to his eye. It was the first time. Slowly he turned and looked upon ridge after ridge of soft dark fir, fading to a pale green glow where the sun had set. *Was there such a thing,* he wondered, *as too much?*

Lady Demaris had supper on the table, and when William arrived they sat and ate. She nodded sadly as Colin explained how Lady Lira had done it again. A single candle flickered pensively in their midst.

"The boy," she mused. "He is new—a fledgling servant of the Lava Beast. His skill will increase. It will go the harder for us."

There was a long silence. The candle shadows ebbed and flowed. William felt the urge to speak.

"I could stay and help," he said to his own surprise. "I mean, I would if you need me to. That is, if I wouldn't be in the way." He nervously scratched the new whiskers on his chin.

Colin beamed. "Good show, man. You'll make a brave song yet."

Lady Demaris still looked thoughtful. She took a scrap of paper out of her smock and smoothed it on the table. "The last time Garth was here," she said, "he left this with me." She pushed the paper across the table to William. "Read it," she told him.

He knew the writing. He slowly read the lines aloud:

> *"Out of the jaws, out of the cave,*
> *Is saved the man that us shall save."*

"That man is you," said Lady Demaris.

William was stunned. His plans were crumbling. "I have a poem too," he confessed. "And a key. They were Garth's." He pulled the key from his pocket and laid it beside the scrap of paper.

Colin whistled. "Now that's upping the ante," he said.

Even Lady Demaris looked surprised. She took the key and studied it closely, holding it up in the candlelight. "This once belonged to my father," she whispered. "He never told us what it opened." She paused. "And the poem?"

"In my pack," said William. He looked around the room. His face fell.

"Sorry, old man," Colin said. "All burnt and shredded, I'm afraid."

"Do you recall it?" asked Lady Demaris. "Any of it?"

"No, not really," he said glumly.

A problematic silence descended. William felt unutterably foolish. "There's someone else," he blurted out. "A girl. She read the poem too."

"The lovely Grace?" asked Colin.

"Yes. I met her at the trailhead. She was lost, I think. I found the poem then and showed it to her. Then she left, and later I met someone looking for her. He told me her name: Grace Foster. For her name's sake I thought she might be some relation to Garth. And from then on I wanted her to help me. But I don't know where she is now. I haven't been able to find her."

Lady Demaris nodded. "Garth has a niece," she said. "He often speaks of her. But in recent years she has made him sad. From what he has told me, I never expected to see her here. But changes are afoot. Perhaps she has come to the mountains at last. Let's hope she comes to us before she comes to Lady Lira. Meanwhile, you must wait for her, William."

"And I for my Rosamond," sighed Colin.

Lady Demaris laughed merrily. "Your Rosamond has her own marmots to tend just now. You too must be patient."

She turned to William again. "So tell us, how did you come by the key and the poem?"

William gazed at the candle and drew a deep breath. The

others settled on their stools. It was the moment most savored of any tale—the moment before it begins, when anything is possible and nothing yet precluded. It was in this moment, as William searched for words to start, that suddenly the door beside them shook with clamor. They all jumped, and William uttered a little shriek. Someone outside was desperately knocking. Before they could move, the door flung open, and in staggered Grace, her wild breath abounding.

12

GRACE COLLAPSED IN THE open door, too winded even to ask who lived here. Seconds later a small marmot shot across the threshold and quivered in her lap. It too was spent. They sat with heads bowed, weary refugees, mother and child.

Lady Demaris was first to rise. She filled a cup with cold water and stooped over the girl. "Drink this, child," she said. "You are welcome here."

Without looking up, Grace took the cup with shaking hands and drained it, gasping. Some of the water fell into her lungs. She coughed violently. The time came to stop, but the spasm went on. The marmot jumped away.

"That's her," said William softly. "That's Grace."

"Lovely indeed," Colin said. "She's had a scare, I think."

At length her coughing departed. Grace felt less exhausted now, but her breath still came hard. She gripped the doorpost and peered outside. The meadow was in starlight. She saw no one out there. Even so, she leapt to her feet and slammed the door.

"Who is chasing you, dear?" asked Lady Demaris.

Somehow Grace did not mind being "dear" to this woman. She risked the truth in reply. "Lady Lira," she panted.

"Beastly woman," muttered Colin.

"Rest yourself, Grace," said Lady Demaris. "You are safe

here. She cannot come in this house anymore." She paused. "Do you recognize any of us?"

Grace wondered that the woman knew her name. Then she saw the man from the trailhead and pointed at him silently.

"Do you remember me, Grace?" he asked.

She nodded. It was awkward for him.

"I'm William—I didn't tell you last time. This is Lady Demaris. And Colin—he lives here too."

Grace nodded to each of them. To her surprise, she even smiled at Lady Demaris, who seated her at the table. The marmot hopped in her lap again.

"I ran into someone looking for you," William explained. "That's how we know your name. We've been hoping you'd come."

That she was expected here in this strange cottage seemed eerie to Grace. "Where's my uncle?" she blurted out. She had not planned to say this.

"I don't know," said William. "I just know where I saw him last. Maybe Lady Demaris has an idea."

Lady Demaris shook her head. "Your uncle will find you when the time is right," she said. "In the meantime, will you help us?"

From anyone else the question would have been untimely. But from Lady Demaris it was the warmest of invitations. Still, Grace wondered if she could trust these strangers. She thought it over. The man from the trailhead, so rude before, now seemed merely nervous, almost considerate. Lady Demaris was motherly enough, and Colin she had noticed was no friend of Lady Lira's. It occurred to Grace that she had to trust someone in these mountains, someone beyond the warm marmot in her lap.

The others remained silent. It had taken William all day to choose; Grace had only minutes. She looked up. "I will help you," she said quietly. Her choice had melted into place before she knew she had made it.

"A brave girl!" cried Colin.

Grace was released like a hemlock that springs from the snowpack in May. It flings the ice clods aside and rocks in the sun. Just so, she basked in the welcome of the three faces. Lady Demaris put hot buttered bread and a bowl of stew before her. Grace ate all of it, except for some morsels she slipped to her marmot. Then she asked what was in the stew, and William found this funny. He laughed very hard, and Grace laughed with him—she didn't know why. They laughed much longer than the joke was worth, and then laughed because they were still laughing, at which point Colin and Lady Demaris laughed too, and the end did not come quickly.

At last—when they could manage it—Lady Demaris served tea all around. At the second cup she touched Grace's arm and said, "Now, child, can you tell us how you came here?"

Grace was only too ready. She scrunched up on her elbows to begin. "It all started," she said, "when I signed up for a trip with You-Can-Do-It Expeditions."

"You can do it?" asked Colin. "You can do *what*?"

"I don't know," said Grace. "I didn't stay long enough to find out."

"Let her tell her story," said Lady Demaris.

Grace went on. They listened patiently until she came to writing down Garth's poem.

"Do you still have it?" asked Lady Demaris.

"Right here," said Grace. She pulled the paper from her jacket and waved it in the air.

"Good girl," said Lady Demaris. "Continue."

They were silent again till she got to the part about Lance going off on the marmot hunt. Then Colin spoke up. "So that's who the little toad was."

"You've seen him?" asked Grace.

"I've laid more than my eyes on him."

"Hush," said Lady Demaris. "We can tell our story later."

But Lady Demaris herself interrupted when Grace told about seeing Garth in the mirror. "You really did see him then? That's good. That's a good sign, dear."

Then Grace told them what Lady Lira had said about snatching an ax—or those it was meant for, and about Lance being "put out of the way." William paled, and Colin slapped the table with last-straw conviction.

Grace realized she had not had time to worry about Lance until now. She turned to Lady Demaris. "What do you think she has done with him?" she asked.

Lady Demaris looked troubled. "Let's hope for the best," she urged.

Grace continued, faltering now, until she reached the shredded pack and the limp mitten at the end of the tunnel.

"That could have been me," said William. "But it wasn't."

"Who was it then?" asked Grace.

"No one," he said. "All that I had. My remains."

Grace puzzled over this. Then she told of the cry far back in the tunnel and of running down a starlit trail that finally led to the cottage.

"That's a good three miles," said Colin. His voice was admiring.

"Again," said Lady Demaris, "welcome, Grace. We are glad you are with us."

William and Colin nodded emphatically.

"Now," she said, "it is your turn, William."

William cleared his throat and promptly set out. For the first time the others heard the full circumstances of Garth's disappearance. Lady Demaris kept nodding as if she had known all along that this was to happen. Even the missing road did not surprise her.

"What did happen to the highway?" William asked her.

"Oh, it comes and goes," she smiled. "It depends who you are."

This did not satisfy William. But he went on describing what he could recall of his night encounter in the cave. For Grace's sake he explained what Lady Demaris had told him about Lady Lira and the Lava Beast.

"Your sister?" Grace said in astonishment. Then, "Why would he ever want to marry *that* woman?" And, "So *those* are the dragons in her house." And, "He eats marmots?" She held her own marmot close to her cheek. He was now fast asleep.

"You have eaten them too, child, if you dined at my sister's house," said Lady Demaris.

Grace felt her stomach revolt.

"How perfectly awful. I—I didn't mean to."

Colin clapped her on the shoulder. "Take heart," he said. "You couldn't have known."

To change the subject—but not by much—he told her about the afternoon marmot raid.

Grace looked at him sharply. "You beat him?" she demanded.

Colin nodded meekly. "I didn't know," he answered.

"He deserved it," Grace said. But suddenly she began to cry. If only Lance had not been "put out of the way," she could hate him freely.

Lady Demaris leaned over and put her arms around Grace. "Poor fool," she said. "Poor, dear, fond fool. Have hope." The woman held the girl, the girl held the marmot, and the marmot awoke to hot tears splashing on his back. Colin grew misty-eyed. William stared blankly at the table. Grace wept as long as she had coughed, which was a long time. When her tears had subsided, she sniffed several times and recomposed herself, humbled and refreshed.

"Sorry," she said.

"You don't have to be sorry," they all replied at once.

Lady Demaris got more tea for everyone. When she sat down again, she pointed to the paper now crushed in Grace's hand. "The poem, child," she said. "I think we should know what your uncle would say to us."

Grace uncrumpled the poem and placed it on the table by William's key and Lady Demaris's slip of rhyme.

Colin saw how long it was. "Can't beat that," he said. "I'm out."

The stanza was carefully traced in the back-slanting script that some girls favor and no one else can read. Since this was the case, Grace read the poem aloud:

> *"A gentle wight for gentle ladies three*
> *Aduentured through a verdant wood newgrowne,*
> *Through wildernesse that mote a wastlond bee,*
> *Vnless he greete the greenwood for his owne,*
> *Vnless he know the leaf as ice and stone.*
> *Faine needs he find a maid of faerie eyne,*
> *To spie the shielde vpon the second throne,*
> *To limn therein the ledgers ancient line—*
> *Lest Beast and woman darke the northerne morning*
> *shyne."*

"Nicely read," said Colin.

"What does it mean in English?" William asked.

Colin eyed him suspiciously. "It *is* in English," he said.

"Shh," said lady Demaris. "Let's see what Grace has to say."

Grace wrinkled her brow and rescanned the poem, musing in silence. Then she had something. "All right. The 'gentle wight,' if I remember correctly, is simply a man—a nice man maybe or a man of noble birth perhaps. He is going on an adventure for the sake of three ladies. But I'm afraid I don't know who these ladies are."

A thought occurred. "You don't have another sister, do you, Lady Demaris?"

"We once did," came the reply, "but she drowned, in a way. It was very peculiar. Perhaps I can tell you more later on."

"I see," Grace said quietly. "Well, that wouldn't fit anyway. Lady Lira couldn't be one of the three, for she is the woman with the beast in the last line—the Lava Beast, most likely. The man must help the ladies by keeping the beast and woman from ruining things, from bringing darkness."

"Why can't the three ladies be our Three Queens?" asked Colin.

"Who?" said Grace.

"Our Three Queens—the mountains we live under."

"I suppose they could be," Grace said, "if there are three of them." She herself did not know if there were three or three hundred.

"I think we've skipped something," said William. "Who is the man?"

The table was still. No one looked up.

William sighed. "I was afraid of that," he said.

"Don't worry," said Grace. "I'm sure you'll make a good wight." She smiled at him hopefully. "And look. It has to be you, William, because what you found at the end of the trail was a 'wood newgrowne.' It is a wilderness, but not a wasteland—apparently there's a difference. But it might become a wasteland if you don't 'greete the greenwood' or 'know the leaf.' What do you suppose that means?"

William looked at the floor.

"William," said Lady Demaris slowly, "do you love this place?"

He stared harder at the floor. He felt cornered. A snarl

began to well beneath the scars on his chest. He looked up, ready to say the whole thing was unfair. But when he met Lady Demaris's green eyes, he recalled the peak in alpenglow, the cold stream running through lupine thickets, the soft forest fading to the western sea. And he simply said, "It's a good place. It is good."

"Long ago that was spoken," said Lady Demaris. "And at some times and in some places, we can almost say it still. Would that we could." She sighed. "William, it is left for us to believe those words have found their truth again. Do you understand that?"

"I think so," said William. He understood not at all.

"You see," she said earnestly, "before this you have grasped only part of the good of the mountains, and in grasping only part you have rejected a great deal else that is good. Get their full tidings, William. When we are given something fair, we must accept and care for all of it. Not that we ourselves can remove the curse—we *are* the curse ourselves. But the curse is fading, in us and around us. Our greatest work is to rest in that hope."

She held his eyes for a long time before turning to Grace. "Go on, child," she told her.

"Well," stammered Grace, "the next thing our wight must do is find a girl with fairy eyes, whoever that is." She had half an idea, but she was not about to volunteer it.

"I think you know," said Lady Demaris. "Your uncle has told me you are like him in many ways. You wouldn't have seen him in the mirror otherwise."

Grace snorted. "Me?" she said. "Do I fly around snatching teeth from under pillows? I'm a girl, not a fairy."

"Most of you is a girl," said Lady Demaris. "But a little bit of you, enough to help us now, is fairy. Anyone who knows can see it in your eyes."

"So they sparkle," said Grace. "Lots of people have eyes

that sparkle." She looked to Colin and William for support. They, in turn, looked to the rafters and lent their support to the roof.

"There's no use pretending you are not who you are," said Lady Demaris.

"You can do it," said Colin.

"Don't worry," said William, "I'm sure you'll make a good fairy."

Grace stuck out her lower lip.

"Go ahead with the poem," said Lady Demaris. "You're doing well."

Grace drew herself up. "This fairy," she said in disgust, "is supposed to look at a shield—or something—on 'the second throne'—wherever that is. See—I have no idea where that could be. It can't be me."

"I'd guess 'the second throne' is the summit of the Center Queen," said Colin. "That's not so hard."

"Well, I have *no* idea how to get up *there*," wailed Grace. "I've never climbed a mountain in my life. I don't even like stairs."

"I know the way," said William calmly.

"Then you don't need me," Grace pouted.

"What does the next line say?" asked Lady Demaris.

She looked. "I think it says there is a book in the throne—that is, on the mountaintop."

"And?" said Lady Demaris.

"And—" She paused. "And that I am to read it." There was defeat in her voice. "But why me? Anyone can read, can't they?"

"There are readers," said Lady Demaris, "and there are readers."

"Okay, okay," said Grace. "So I go up there and read this book. But then what do we do?"

"I don't know," said Lady Demaris, "but you know what to do now."

"What about Lance? We can't just leave him, can we?"

"The surest way to find him, dear, is to follow the poem. You can't weaken my sister's hold any other way, I'm afraid."

Grace shrugged her shoulders. She was out of objections. She would not look at William. "So when do we leave?" she finally said, as if any one time were as bad as another.

"You must go before dawn," said Lady Demaris. "My sister knows you are here and will return at sunrise. Meanwhile, she has no doubt left some of her own to watch us. You must try to elude them when it is dark. We must get you ready—it is now past midnight. The moon will soon rise."

Lady Demaris got up from the table, and so did everyone else. Grace and William shared a glance. For all their reluctance they now felt slightly important. They stood shyly together while Colin poured out a cascade of gear from the loft—boots and ropes and packs and caps and mittens and knickers and candles and lanterns. For their feet he tossed down iron-clawed creepers that crashed to the floor. Lady Demaris came to Grace with sweaters and coats, saying, "Here, try this on. Perfect fit, dear." At one point she put a small wooden ice ax in her hand and whispered, "My younger sister's. She would have wanted you to have it."

When all was ready, William and Grace were transformed. Grace had exchanged her shorts for green woolen knickers which reached to the top of Lady Lira's boots. A thick olive sweater replaced her jacket, which was now compressed in a canvas rucksack. William wore hobnailed boots that clattered on the floor and knickers and kneesocks of coarse gray wool. Beside him leaned a drab packsack on a wooden frame. It had neither zippers nor compartments, and it smelled distinctly of hot bread.

"One more thing," said Lady Demaris. She fetched from

a corner another ice ax, battered and smooth, and handed it to William. "This belonged to my father, Lord Linton, who built this cottage long ago. With this ax he was first to climb all three of our Queens. The shaft was cut from an ash tree many miles to the north, farther north than any other ash tree grows. The tree yet stands, and when the wind blows in that northern vale, the ax still trembles. You will feel it."

William felt it. His hand shook nervously.

"Use my father's ax for now," she said. "There is only one better."

Out one window the quarter moon began to rise, rimmed by the peak of the Center Queen. They blew out the candles and waited in silvered darkness, hoping that anyone watching the cottage would think they had turned in. The air smelled late in the candle smoke. Everything felt strangely still. Getting ready was easy. Being ready was hard. The quietness held doubts.

Grace began to yawn, and then she felt the wet poke of a marmot nose in her hand. She stroked the marmot's head. "I wish you were going," she whispered.

"He should go," said Lady Demaris. "What you cannot see, he can smell. These days, a good marmot is hard to find."

Grace was glad. "You hear that?" she told the marmot. "You're coming with us." She pressed him against her knees.

Then Lady Demaris opened the door, and the raw cold rushed in.

13

THE THREE CLIMBED SOFTLY up moonlit meadows. Grace kept close on William's heels, the marmot close on hers. Wet grass wrapped and clung to their feet, a breeze cooled their faces. Island clumps of mountain hemlock—sure to hold unfriendly spies—loomed and passed them by. But neither whistle nor whisper broke the night. They hoped they walked unseen, unsniffed, on their way to the mountain.

In time, the hemlock clumps grew small and sparse, the air sharper. The dewy grass released their steps and shrank in frosty manicure. There were terraces where little streams stopped in silvered pools tinged with borders of thinnest ice. Deep in their waters, miles deep in crystal darkness, shone all the stars of heaven.

Then came piles of stony rubble, snaking into the meadows. The climbers wandered up grassy halls until the grass gave out. They hopped from boulder to boulder then and stopped at the foot of a steep rock mound. Grace's breath echoed in her ears. Her nose was dripping. If William had not paused just then, she would have spoken up.

"Last moraine," he whispered.

Grace looked at the sky. "Doesn't look like any more rain to me," she said. "Plenty of stars."

"No, this," he answered, tapping the rocks with his ax. "The glacier piled it here. We've got to climb over to get to the snow. Be very careful. Stay beside me, not behind me—I might kick something loose."

Grace nodded.

"And keep your ax away from the rocks. No use battering it up worse than it already is."

Grace nodded again. Before she was ready, William started up, and she had to scramble after. It wasn't easy, for very few of the stones stayed put—they clunked and teetered underfoot as if randomly piled one atop the other, which they were. Only the marmot, light on his feet, passed undisturbing and undisturbed. The moraine was loose—so loose that with each new step Grace feared she would trigger a massive rock slide. And halfway up, she did. She had no sooner mounted the uptilted edge of a large flat stone than it swung shut like the lid of a trunk. As it scooted away, she leapt to the side, trembled, watched. The stone ponderously upended itself, hung for an instant poised in the night, then tumbled on, recruiting whole armies of boulders for the charge. The clatter was immense, like the smashing of giant dishes. Grace saw sparks as rock broke upon rock—and smelt them too. William watched beside her as the noise faded, died in the darkness.

"Do you think they heard?" she asked.

As if in answer, a whistle pierced the night below them. Then came another, faraway, and a third, more distant still. Grace felt with her hand for her own little marmot, worried he might have been caught in the rockfall. He was safe at her side. But his body was quaking beneath her mitten, just as it had beneath the bed of Lady Lira. The whistling repeated itself in the distance; the marmot went absolutely rigid.

"He's frightened," she said. "What he hears, he knows." Her heart sank—in part at the prospect of fewer rest stops.

William shrugged. "Guess we better move on," he replied. He was almost glad for the excuse to climb quickly.

And so they tiptoed up the moraine—like barefoot children on hot asphalt—and this time left each stone unturned. From the crest they hopped a short ways down the other side to a long snowshore. The snow was rippled, frozen hard.

William shed his pack. "Out with the irons," he said. "I'll uncoil the rope."

Grace gaped at the rise of glacier ahead. It swept toward them, all of a piece, one vast pouring of ice. It seemed to her like the white train of a wedding gown. But unlike a bridal train, its icy fabric was scissored and torn. Crevasses were plentiful.

"How do we get through those?" she asked, pointing.

"Mostly we walk around them," he told her. "Sometimes there are bridges of snow."

Grace wondered why bridges of snow should hold when piles of rocks did not. William, meanwhile, strapped the iron claws to her feet and tied the end of a rope about her waist. The rope was braided and rough and hairy—she could feel it through her mittens. William was tied to the other end.

"This way I hold you if you fall," he explained.

"What if you fall?" Grace shot back.

"I won't," he assured her. "But if I do, you stop me with your ax."

Grace looked askance at the bladed pick of the ice ax in her hand. "My aim is pretty bad," she said. "Besides that, it would probably hurt." She pictured William safely impaled on the lip of a crevasse.

"Not that way," William replied. "Throw yourself down and dig your ax into the snow. Then the rope stops me." He lay facedown and demonstrated. "You should probably try it," he told her.

Grace watched him grovel in the cold hard snow. It looked very uncomfortable. "I don't think there's time," she said. "Shouldn't we be going—like, in case we're being followed?"

William was dubious of her motives, but he gave in and got up. Before setting out he merely made sure that she held the ax head properly—thumb beneath the adze, fingers curled over the pick.

They were not a perfect rope team. Grace followed William by some sixty feet. Though her iron creepers bit down well, they heavily weighed her steps. Her pace soon slackened, and the rope jerked taut on her waist. At just this moment the rope stopped William in midstride. He was no more pleased than a dog on a leash, nor Grace than its owner pulled behind. After many such moments, each suspected the other of venting some spite, and what began by chance proceeded by malice. William walked in quick bursts to catch her by surprise. Grace, equally crafty, let coils of slack drift out of her hand, and then dug in her heels to watch him bounce on the end of his tether. The marmot was fortunate. Without a rope, he walked unmolested in natural innocence.

At the first hint of dawn, William stopped at the lip of a real crevasse—the largest so far. Grace caught up to him, prepared to deliver her withering stare. But instead she looked down. The ice walls plunged to a cavernous trench. They were white at the top, then faintly blue, then lost in black below. She saw no bottom. One slip and she would be lost to the world. She looked up, awestruck.

William had his pack off, and he gruffly handed her bread and water. She sat down on her rucksack and tried to eat, but had no stomach for it. She shivered a bit, patted her marmot, and told him not to fall in the hole.

William overheard. "A crevasse," he said. "Not a 'hole.'"

Meanwhile, the dawn gathered around them. The glacier blushed a faint rose tinge that deepened by the minute. They were high enough, and it was light enough, to see to the moraines, tossed up like earthworks against a siege. Below stretched the meadows, waking into color, and they even saw a tiny dot for the cottage whence they came. Westward surged forest, soft and dark, reaching whole and entire to the morning star, bright beneath the dusky moon. Grace did not know that the normal vista was of patchy brown checkers, tiered with roads. She did not know that shining Venus was often lost in a brown haze. But William knew. And unaware, he blessed all that was below him.

The glacier was fully flushed now, and the summit of the North Queen, visible to one side, burned gold in direct sunlight. They saw it and put on their packs. Most of the glacier remained to climb.

William led off around the crevasse to where it pinched away. Grace was about to follow when she heard something. It was a faraway tintinnabulation, like a wind chime in a faint breeze. The marmot stopped still, and she heard the tinkling sound again. Then she spied small puffs of gray, floating up from the nearest moraine. Tiny figures scuttled onto the lap of the glacier. One was much larger than the others.

"Look," said Grace. She pointed.

William saw, and he groaned. They were not much more than an hour ahead. "Can you go any faster?" he called back.

He set off, and she answered with her feet. The rope quivered more evenly now. Their creepers sliced in better rhythm. Crevasses slipped by, on right, on left, some beneath winding bridges of snow. Once Grace leapt from lip to lip, the marmot tucked in her arms. Compared to Lady Lira, crevasses were friendly.

Soon William led them through upreared towers of banded ice—a maze of seracs. They shone turquoise and gold in the dawn. He wound steeply between them, chopping steps with his adze in close succession. Shavings of ice sprayed out from his ax into morning light. Grace followed quickly, clawing each of her feet into place, and the marmot swiftly bounded behind, dragging his tail up the steps.

From out of the seracs they emerged upon a sloping snowfield. It was dazzling white, and the sky burned blue. Only one more crevasse now crossed their way. The largest yet—the bergschrund. It would require a long end run.

"Can you see them?" called William. He sounded anxious.

Grace looked back, breathing heavily. She could only see the tumble of seracs. As she began to reply, she heard a sound, not a jingling of rocks this time but a stifled groaning of ice. Under her feet the glacier shuddered, shifting within. Then down the slope, in slowest motion a serac no smaller than a Stonehenge stone gave way and exploded across their tracks. Shivering chunks of ice flew up and powdered the air in clouds of crystal. Grace stared agawk at the settling powder.

William came down and put a hand on her shoulder. "That'll hold 'em up," he said. He tried to sound as if falling seracs were something that came his way each morning. But his hand was shaking.

The summit was nigh. It would not serve to only stand and quake. They traversed the bergschrund far to the right, circled the end, and marched directly up steep white slopes. Feathers of ice now brushed their boots, and the air stabbed a chill in their lungs. William's face was clammy white. Grace was starting to wobble. Their hearts were racing much faster than their feet. But their axes plunged on, steadily on, as if separately empowered.

Grace believed that, just ahead, the slope would level out. But "just ahead" was most unjust—it kept on receding. Her breath came wildly. Her feet splayed here and stumbled there. She bargained with the mountain for fifty more steps, then fifty more. The bargain, she decided, was not worth renewing. So Grace caved in, draping herself on the head of her ax like a towel thrown over the back of a chair.

"Sorry," she wheezed. "Gotta stop."

William looked back. "Almost there," he said weakly. He peered below and thought he saw movement by the first large crevasse. But he wasn't sure. He gave Grace a minute to recover. Then he pulled gently on the rope. "Not much farther," he called down.

Grace had not really caught her breath but followed anyway, dragging a bit on the end of her leash but too dizzy to care. Then, suddenly, the slope began to ease. In a few steps more it leveled completely. This was the top. No, this was not the top. William had not stopped. He was plodding towards a rocky nub in the midst of a snowy plain. The nub was far away. Grace felt cheated, but staggered on. Like a mirage, the rocky nubbin kept its distance. It mocked all notion of progress. She gave up watching the summit rock and fell once more to counting steps. At exactly two hundred she peeked—and regretted it. At two hundred more she looked again and saw enough to hope by. Six hundred steps and there it was—she'd caught the summit napping. William was at the rock now. He scrambled up and turned to reel her in. Grace stepped from the snow, balanced up beneath him. Her creepers skated on stony ledges; the shaft of her ice ax bumped and banged. At William's feet she dropped the ax. And collapsed.

"Is this it?" she moaned. The marmot was licking her face.

"The very place," he answered proudly. "Too bad my watch is busted—I think we made it in record time." He paused to regard her. "You did all right, you know."

Exhausted as she was, Grace still felt the full force of this compliment. She lifted her head. "Thanks," she panted. "Thanks a lot." She thought of her long-lost Lance Q. Lott and began to examine the far-flung view.

William checked her. "The book should be in there," he said, pointing to a silver box beside them. "Let's take a quick look."

He crouched over the box to unfasten the screwclamps. To his surprise, there were none. He inspected the lid closely. Instead of the stamped logo of his alpine club, it framed a curiously engraved picture. The detail was exquisite. He saw a graceful mountain draped with ice. Below it were tottering moraines, rolling meadows, streams, flowers, marmots playing—even deer standing shyly at the edge of the forest. The entire picture was no larger than a hand-held shield, but in whatever place he looked, William could make out as much detail as he liked, down to the whisker of a marmot.

He motioned to Grace, speechless.

She knelt beside him and followed his eyes to the lid of the box. The first thing she saw was a cottage in the meadows. The front door was open to let in the sun. Then she caught her breath. Out of the door in the picture walked a woman. Her face was easy to recognize.

"Look!" said Grace. "It's Lady Demaris!"

William followed her finger. "I don't see her," he said.

"Right there!" Grace insisted. "She's looking up at the mountain now. She seems very worried."

William eyed the girl suspiciously.

"And look here, down the stream," she continued. "It's Colin, tending the marmots. I think he's singing."

William could not see Colin either. "Are you making this up?" he demanded.

Grace wasn't listening. "And here," she said. "You can see our tracks up the side of the mountain. Right there is where the ice fell over."

Suddenly she began to shake. "And there's Lady Lira," she whispered. "And her marmots. I can see her face—her eyes even." Grace had to look away. The woman's eyes were fixed on her, cold as malice congealed.

"Where are they?" urged William.

She braced herself for another look. "They're in the ice

towers now. She's got one, two, five, six—let me see—ten marmots with her. And in her hand she has—" Grace stopped, barely able to say what she saw, "a dagger."

They looked at one another, and William tittered nervously. He would never be able to explain why.

"The book," said Grace. "Maybe we can take it with us down the other side."

"There aren't any screws," William said flatly. He pried at the lid in vain. "I don't know how it opens."

Grace inspected the sides of the box. On the front she saw a keyhole. She pointed silently.

"Worth a try," William agreed. He wished that he had seen it first. He bit off one mitten and snatched the rusty key from his pocket. It fit perfectly. He turned it. As if by magic, the lid arose.

Within lay a folio ledger, old and scuffed and leather-bound. The edges of the leaves showed ragged and yellow. Grace very carefully scooped it up, but the book tugged back like a partner on a rope. She felt underneath it. The spine was fastened to the box by a chain—and the box itself was immovably fixed in the summit rock. The book was not for borrowing. She looked up at William.

"We have a while anyway," he said, shrugging his shoulders. "Read what you can, and we'll slide down the backside soon enough."

To Grace this felt like a timed examination, except much worse. Exams could sometimes make her ill, and her stomach right now was poised on the verge. She told herself to calm down. She took a deep breath, and the alpine pungence ached in her nostrils. Then, with trembling mitten, she pawed the cover open.

The first thing she saw was a huge single letter—an *L*—at the top of the page. The letter was green and well-adorned with boughs of fir and tumbling marmots. She smiled faintly to herself. But beneath the green *L* stretched a column of stanzas in antique angular script. It was poetry. Her heart dropped. She flipped through page after page of relentless verse, and hope decayed with each falling leaf. How could she read it all?

Midway through the book, partway down one brittle page, the writing abruptly stopped. She swiftly checked the remaining pages—all were blank. So she glanced back at the final stanza and read the final line:

> Lest Beast and woman darke the northerne morning
> shyne.

In quick surprise she skimmed the lines above. To the word it was her uncle's poem, now only part of a poem partly written. But this part she already knew—there was no use dwelling here. So she paged toward the front of the book once more.

"Where do I start?" she whined aloud.

"Beats me," said William. He was nervously checking the snowy plain at the place where their steps met the sky.

In despair, Grace returned to the first page. After she got a start on it, maybe she could skip around.

Here is how the book began:

> Lo here the mount where Muses faine would dwell,
> Forwearied of Parnassus grimie hill,
> Forsaking Helicons heat-parched well
> For fountains of green ice that higher spill.
> Lo these the mountains, these my song shall fill
> To ouerflowing with deepe historie.
> Reeds oaten, trumpets sterne, use that ye will:
> Both fitting bee to blazon to the skie
> Braue deeds of maids and men lest praise of them may
> die.

Help then, O Muses, here awaited long—
Ye welcome bee farre flown across the seas.
Vnwearied now renew an alpine song,
Blow forth glad breath and sweete the vernall breeze;
Make autumn gales my falt'ring notes to seize.
Three Queenes here reign your seruice to demand;
Three Queenes require your seruice, ye thrice three,
To sing the heroes in their high command
That laboured haue long time to green a groning land.

    Gag me! thought Grace. *Gag the Muses! If there's a story,* let's get on with it.

    She skipped several pages and read on in a hurry:

So he expelled was from that green world;
To loue and tend vnwilling had he beene.
Mosquitoes now before the portal whirl'd
Hot deadlie needles, guarding all the green.
He once that honor'd euery verdant Queene,
Now hurl'd in dusty exile selfe-impos'd
For plucking that was pleasant to bee seene:
Not keeper he but taker was expos'd
When rounde the trembling fruite his grasping fingers
    clos'd.

Now out, he best considers his reuenge,
How most to quyte the place he cannot in.
Full sorelie he desireth to auenge
Him that would say his new-wonne knowledge sinne.
For now his eies are open that had been
To wisdom clos'd: that trees may build a towre,
That meadows are most ripe of gold within,
That rivers damm'd churn glorie into powre.
The verie grapes that grow, but for him would bee
    soure.

So pricking to and fro he seeks a waie
The arbor vitae he may haply smite.
From dust to dust he faine would sift the clay;
To life in death fower rivers he would spyte.
But grutching he remaynes vntill the night,
For much he fears the dread mosquitoe sting;
Their fatal poyson he can no-wise fight.
The hallow'd ground they adamantly ring;
Full thicke they thirst for blood, full angry they doe
    sing.

Almost the wight was given to despayr,
When lo, a monstrous forme, by hidden heast,
'Gan suddeinly seepe vp into the ayre
From out the ground in trickling bloodie yeast
That gurgl'd darke—and griesly it increast.
Full gracelesse shape it tooke, of filthie hue
And fearfull was its name: The Lava Beast.
All bloated was its maw with magma stewe
That dript downe from its iaws, and from its nostrills
    too.

Addressing then it selfe vnto the man,
It spoke in fire and breathed smokie ashe:
Ye wish (quoth it) to enter if ye can
Where one surcharg'd of surquedry so rash
Did whip thee hence with cruell mosquitoe lash.
Unfairly is the land lockt vp in paine
Agaynst thy needfull use—ye rightly gnash
Thy teeth to lose that ought to be thy gaine.
Thy manhoode bears a slight, thine honor suffers
    staine.

Now hearken thou to me, areed my words,
For I can ye most excellently ayde
To penetrate yon thicke mosquitoe herds

Unharm'd, unstung, unscath'd, and well ypaide
By vse compleat of all before thee layd.
For nought can yon mosquitoes bear my fire,
And 'fore my smoke they quick disperse and fayd.
All needs ye doen is join ye to mine hire:
Staie fast by me alway, and 'scape the buggy ire.

Fear not (it said), I stronger am than he
That would vpon thee place a feeble hex.
And if he gave it thought he'd certes see
That what he wrought in thee he cannot vex—
Created to subdue: Domini lex!
Subdue? Yea, haue dominion he did say,
Reign lord o'er all the land, tyrannus rex!
What think ye now? Wouldst thou hold all in sway?
Join then thyself to me: I only am the waie.

Right glad the wight receiued this aduice;
To all the Beast did say he well did harke—
In fine, he made the bargayn in a trice.
Vpon his hart the Beast then sear'd a marke,
With inly marke his hart made flamy darke;
Not on the foreheade as it has been tolde,
But deepe within a fest'ring smokie spark.
By this the Beast brought him into his folde:
Now easie to bee bought, but harder to be solde.

Grace stopped again. William was drumming on the lid of the box.

"So what are we supposed to do?" he asked. "Did you find out?"

"There's a few things here about the Lava Beast," she said, "but nothing real helpful so far. It's a poem that tells a story. I can't begin to read it all."

William sliced at the rock with his heel. They should have been gone by now.

Grace had her own thoughts. "William," she quavered, "when you met the Lava Beast, he didn't talk to you, did he?"

"Nope," said William.

"So you never talked to him either?"

"Are you kidding? I was barely awake. Besides, I was busy." He paused. "Look at that lid again, will you? See if you can spot her."

Grace looked. Lady Lira was through the seracs and striding over the final bergschrund. Fewer marmots were at her side—she must have outdistanced the slow ones.

Grace pointed to the spot on the picture.

"Time to head out," William declared.

Grace closed the book and replaced it flat in the box. She felt as if she were turning in a far-from-finished essay. She reached for the lid reluctantly and sighed. Then something strange occurred. Till now the marmot had roamed the summit, testing the air with upheld whiskers. But suddenly he bolted towards them and jumped in the box atop the book.

"Get out, silly marmot," said Grace. "We're leaving."

The marmot would not budge.

"Scat," said William.

The marmot remained. Grace tried to pick him up—he scratched her. William tried to swat him out—he bared his teeth.

"Let's go," said William. "It'll follow us."

"But we can't leave the lid up," said Grace. "I don't think Lady Lira should touch this book."

"Better the book than us," huffed William.

He clambered off the rocks and began tromping east, away from their tracks. Grace watched the rope slither out from her feet. It was almost uncoiled when she heard a sharp whistle. William stopped. Grace saw them first—three silhouettes on the eastern horizon. They all were galloping straight for William. At the very same time, three more marmots emerged on the north.

"Come back!" she shouted.

She reeled him in frantically. He stumbled towards her, a clumsy fish. Now she checked the south—yet three more were over the edge, running her way.

"Hurry!" she called.

Grace hauled him to the rock, and he flopped onshore. She glanced behind. A giant of a woman raced over their tracks, taking one step for their two. In her hand she held a dagger aloft, and a single marmot dogged her heels.

William stood panting at Grace's side. He turned slowly around and marked each approaching party. But his eyes returned to the woman. "Looks like we use these bloody axes," he whimpered. He wondered if dispatching a marmot would require a perfect golf swing. He had not golfed in years.

"Untie from the rope," he told Grace. "Stay up on these rocks. Remember you can kick the little buggers with your spikes."

Grace took off her mittens and tried to untie the knot at her waist. Her fingers, however, hung limp on the rope. The marmot began to rub her legs like a cat that wants attention. But Grace kept her eyes on the closing attackers. In a minute or so they would all arrive, and then what? She could see the eyes and teeth of the nearest marmots, the quivering lips of Lady Lira. A black gown swept behind the woman; a black hood cowled her face. Her white hand held the dagger high—a flag and a standard ready to strike.

Grace felt another furry nudge on her leg, and this time she looked down. The marmot had upended the book. He was pawing at something on the bottom of the box. Halfheartedly, Grace looked inside. Where the book had been was another keyhole.

"William," she said. "The key!" She tried to shout it but only whispered.

"Hmm?"

"The key!" This was a real shout.

"If you want it," he murmured. His eyes were still on Lady Lira, gliding closer with appalling strength. He held the key out listlessly.

Grace snatched the key and shoved its teeth in the new hole. It smoothly fit and smoothly turned. This time, the entire box unhinged from the rock, swinging up like a thick trap door. Underneath was an open shaft, wide as her shoulders. Steep cut steps—a ladder, almost—led down into darkness.

"In here!" cried Grace. She quickly tossed their packs in the hole.

William revolved in a trance. His lower lip was sagging. He gazed at the shaft as if miles away.

Grace dropped in her ice ax next. It clanked and echoed—a noisy penny in a wishing well. The marmot dove in after it. Then, after closing the book inside its box, Grace squirmed down the hatch herself. Her creepers struck sparks on the hard stone steps.

Very slowly, William gathered up the rope and dumped it in on top of her. He looked to the west. Lady Lira's outstretched hand now touched the rocks below him. He looked north and east—the marmots too had left the snow. He turned south—and a rush of fur sprang snarling upon him. His ice ax dipped and swung on the tee, just as he had imagined. He sliced it. One soft thud and the marmot flew in a gentle arc, touching down on the white fairway. William wondered stupidly at the warm blood dripping from his adze.

"Get in here!" hissed a voice from below.

Clutching his ax, he wriggled in waist-deep and with one hand grasped the edge of the box. It swung down sweetly over his head. But just as he released it, a white-hot slash tore into his hand. He squealed in pain. Then the silver shield clicked shut. It was utterly dark.

14

"CAN WE PLEASE STOP?" It was Jennifer who asked. The pack straps cut her shoulders cruelly. Her hands hung numb, the knuckles puffy with pooled blood.

"We just started," Arnie said firmly. "We can't stop yet." He snorted to show it could not be otherwise.

Arnie was hiking in front today, hunkered beneath a burden meet for a camel with gifts from the Queen of Sheba. His pockets were stuffed with obsidian chips, and each hand held two large mushrooms. Jennifer was breathing in gulps at Arnie's heels. Then came Ronald, his nylon glasses slipping down to the end of his nose. Had it not turned up at the end like a ski jump, his glasses would have long since fallen to the trail, there to be crushed by the tottering steps of the two girls behind him. They slurped the air more raggedly than Jennifer, if possible. The girls were passing a paisley bandana back and forth, each, in turn, tragically stroking the sweat from her brow. The gesture came easily at midday—the hour of soap operas now sorely missed.

Trailing the two girls was the red-bearded young man. He had enthroned Arnie as Leader for the Day, which meant that he himself could placidly observe the agony and the anarchy while dawdling in the rear. This was called Non-Directive Leadership. He was quite good at it. At present he had begun to notice that Jennifer would be most delighted to bury her ax six inches deep in Arnie's skull. This he recognized as Group Process. He would skillfully manage it by refraining from any intervention whatsoever. Only then could the group members reach a Genuine Consensus, preparing themselves not only to function harmoniously at later stages of the expedition, but to mature as assertive yet cooperative individuals in Society at Large. Besides, hiking solo in the rear gave the leader ample time to memorize the immortal verse of Robert Service—no small passion of his:

> When you're lost in the Wild, and you're scared as a
>   child,
> And Death looks you bang in the eye,
> And you're sore as a boil, it's according to Hoyle
> To cock your revolver and . . .

"Please, stop," wheezed Jennifer, and suddenly she did. Ronald crashed into the back of her pack, and apologized. But Arnie walked on, determined, a shepherd without his sheep. Soon, however, the silence at his heels grew suspect. He turned around. Some distance behind him, four carcasses were scattered about as if thrown by a seismic blast. Arnie dropped his mushrooms.

"Hey, I didn't say you could stop!"

"Outvoted," said Jennifer. She lay open-mouthed and panting, her wide eyes pinned to the sky as if dazzled by an angel vision.

Arnie appealed to the red-bearded one, who stood a little ways back. "Hey, I never said they could stop. I'm the leader, aren't I?"

The leader nodded vaguely and walked down the trail to relieve himself. Desertion was mounting. Arnie looked to his friend and ally.

"Why'd you quit, Ronald?" he demanded.

Ronald looked at Jennifer. "I don't know. Tired, I guess."

Arnie rejoined them and took off his pack with manly disgust. He stood over his prostrate followers. "What a bunch of woosies!"

No one denied this.

"I'm the one with the heaviest pack," he said, thumbing his chest. "I got all the gorp, all the lunches, the rope, the stove, all of the gas—"

"You've got all the gas all right," said Jennifer.

Ronald thought this uproarious. He laughed in little hiccups.

One of the girls turned to her friend. "Can you get my water out?"

"Mine too," said Jennifer to Ronald.

The plastic bottles were duly extracted, and inspection revealed a dead fly floating inside the first. The two girls shrieked in unison. One held the bottle at arm's length and dumped the water out.

"Afraid of a little fly?" said Arnie.

No one answered him.

Then Ronald asked for some gorp.

"I'm saving it," said Arnie. He got out his map instead and pondered it alone. This seemed like a leaderly thing to do. As it happened, his study was repaid.

"Hey!" he announced. "The map shows a cabin just down the trail. I'm serious, look."

No one got up.

"Maybe you could bring the map over here," said Ronald.

Arnie scowled but came over. He spread out the map between Ronald and Jennifer. The other two girls sat apart, brushing their hair. Arnie stubbed down his finger on a tiny black square by a thin dotted line. The square was labeled "Demaris Cabin."

"How far?" said Jennifer.

Arnie seized the reins of leadership. "Maybe a mile. If we leave now, we could get there by lunch—have lunch at the cabin."

"But it's time for lunch now."

"I think it'll be worth waiting . . . lunch at the cabin, you know."

At this point the red-bearded leader returned and was asked to arbitrate this most crucial of the day's choices. Normally he respected the Group Decision-Making Process, carefully playing the part of a blank wall which impartially rebounds wayward tennis balls. But in this matter, for special reasons, he deigned to intervene.

"How about the cabin?" he said. The leader well knew that whatever he asked was not really a question.

As it turned out, the cabin lay more than a mile away—at least Jennifer said so when they got there. It sat slightly uphill from the trail, in a meadow next to a stream that leapt down from the Center Queen. The walls were made of blocks of lava fitted together in a crude puzzle. The roof peaked high in bleached and splintered shingles. Some of the shingles littered the beaten ground by the door like broken teeth of a dragon. The door stood ajar, disclosing shade and coolness and mystery. From a pack-laden vantage on the dusty path, it was the door to heaven.

"Can we go in?" asked Arnie. "Does this Demaris guy still live here?"

"Not anymore," said the leader. "Just the back country ranger—when she's not on patrol."

The leader routed his groups this way whenever he could. Right now he wished with all his heart that the ranger would be in. As if wishes were binding, there appeared at the door a comely young woman, blonde and sunburnt. He waved to the woman cautiously, hoping he was remembered.

"Hello!" she called. Her voice fell upon them like haloes

of spray. "I thought you'd be coming. I have huckleberries for you! Come in, won't you? Come in where it's cool."

The group balked, wonder-struck. Then they advanced very shyly, like squirrels approaching a hand-held peanut. At the ranger's direction they parked their packs against the wall and timidly edged through the door. It was indeed cool inside. She sat them around a rough-hewn table that held a bowl of berries. Arnie snagged the first handful.

"Look at that attic," he said, pointing to a loft. "Do you sleep up there?"

"When it rains," said the ranger. "But I usually sleep outside." She flipped a thick blonde braid behind her and took a seat at the head of the table.

"If I lived here, I'd never go outside," said Arnie. "Except when I went climbing."

"So you're a climber?" she said, her green eyes wide with appreciation.

"Yeah. South Queen. Yesterday. Piece o' cake." The truth came out in huckleberry fragments.

"How did the rest of you like it?"

"Fun," said Ronald modestly.

"Most of it," said Jennifer.

"Uh-uh, my feet got cold," said one girl.

"Too far," said the other.

"The best part was comin' back," Arnie added. "I just put on my rain pants and sat down and like, I was gone! I'd climb all the way up there just to slide down again. They should build a lift or something."

"They might," said the ranger.

"Really?" said Arnie.

"What do you mean?" said the leader. It was news to him.

"Ah," she replied. She hunched forward. This creased her khaki uniform shirt and set her badge askew. "So you haven't heard. Well. Bring in your lunch then—I'll tell you."

Jennifer went outside to fetch the lunch from their packs. She found a melting block of cheese and a smashed box of crackers. "Arnie, where's the gorp?" she called.

"Forget it," said Arnie. "Let's just eat. I wanna hear about the chairlift." He took a terrific drag from his water bottle and settled forward on his elbows, a full conspirator with the ranger. She waited for Jennifer and then began.

"Do you remember the creek you hiked up on your first day—Lost Creek?"

They remembered.

"You should see the blister Arnie got there," said Ronald.

"I didn't get no blister," said Arnie.

"That whole drainage—up to the meadows—lies just outside the wilderness boundary," said the ranger.

The leader nodded. He knew that.

"Who's got a knife for the cheese?" said Jennifer.

From under the table the ranger produced a knife with the heft of a dagger.

"Thanks," said Jennifer. "That'll work great."

"Now for years," said the ranger, "they've wanted to build a road and cut the trees along Lost Creek."

"But that's in the courts, isn't it?" asked the leader.

"It was," she answered. "But the final appeal was denied last week. They start on the road next summer."

"Who's 'they'?" asked Ronald.

The ranger paused. "It's us," she answered. "'They' is us."

"I see," said Ronald vaguely.

"The road will go almost to the meadows beneath the South Queen. They may push it a little farther to accommodate a drive-in campground with a splendid view of the mountain." She looked and smiled at the red-bearded leader. "This," she added, "is but one example of the way in which timber harvesting opens up diverse recreational opportunities."

The leader greatly admired her way of putting things.

"Will the campground have showers?" asked one girl. "That might make it worth coming."

"That's the next part," said the ranger. "The campground may have *hot* showers."

"That would be *so* wonderful," said the other girl. "I haven't had a shower in four days. If my mother saw me now, she'd make me take a bath with the dog in the garage."

"Except the dog wouldn't be able to stand it!" shouted Arnie. He held up his nose between his fingers, coating it generously with cheese.

"What are you getting at?" the leader said.

"Okay," said the ranger. She surveyed her pupils. "Do any of you know how the Three Queens got here?"

Ronald felt a summons to speak the truth. "God made them," he said huskily. He felt his face burn.

"Maybe there weren't enough kings to go around," said Arnie. He sputtered crackers on the table in front of him.

The ranger addressed Ronald. "Yes, but how did he—ah—or what kind of mountains are they?"

Ronald lit up. "They're volcanoes."

"Right," said the ranger. "And what makes volcanoes erupt?"

This put Ronald on home ground. "Gasses inside the earth. They get superheated under high pressure and force up magma to the surface. That's the quiet kind of eruption. In the violent kind, the gasses themselves explode into the air, spreading huge clouds of ash and cinders."

Jennifer's gaze spilled admiration.

"Good," said the ranger. "Now. These three volcanoes haven't erupted for hundreds of years, but they're still quite active. In fact, if you climb the North Queen, you'll find sulphur vents below the summit. They shoot out hot steam and smell like someone who likes baked beans."

She waited for Arnie to stop giggling.

"So even though these peaks are covered with snow, they're actually pretty warm underneath—and all of that heat is a valuable resource. For a long time, people have wanted to drill deep holes in the meadows up here and pipe away steam and hot water. Most of the places they've wanted to try are inside the wilderness boundary. That means they can't drill there. But the Lost Creek road will pave the way to a corner of the meadows just outside the designated wilderness. When the road is finished, the drillers will come. In fact, if it weren't for the lawsuits, they would have come by helicopter long ago.

"Anyway, when they find a little, they'll wish for more. So to help things along, they will urge the government to quietly relax a few minor management constraints upon test drilling in the wilderness itself. Their motives, of course, will be solely patriotic: we must inventory our energy resources against all future national emergencies. The government will eventually agree, for we obviously need to meet our country's growing energy needs. Anyone who thinks otherwise does not want our nation to be great. Anyone who thinks otherwise deserves to freeze in the dark."

"Let's have some of those crackers down here," said Arnie.

"You've *had* yours," hissed Jennifer.

"For several summers, helicopters will visit the timberline meadows, bringing in equipment for more test sites. And once a profitable amount of geothermal energy is discovered, an urgent national need for it will suddenly arise. Soon the Three Queens will radiate a full network of pipes, like a giant furnace in the basement of an old house. To construct and maintain these pipelines, roads will be built up virtually every drainage. These roads, of course, will be carefully designed so as not to compromise the wilderness quality of the area."

"How could that be?" asked Ronald.

"She's kidding," said Jennifer.

"No, good point," said the ranger. "For once the roads and wells and pipelines are in place, perceptive legislators will recognize, in all fairness, that this area is no longer wilderness—that to so call such a place after it has been accessed for our emergency energy needs would be a sham, an embarrassment, a stumbling block to the integrity of the wilderness ideal and to the vitality of the rich frontier heritage so dear to our nation. So in a bold move to protect the remaining wilderness in our country, the Three Queens will be subject to revisionary legislation that will entail minor boundary adjustments. The summits themselves will of course retain their wilderness character and classification. But the parameters of management flexibility will be happily enlarged for the rest of the region."

"I'm lost," whispered Jennifer.

"Me too," said Ronald.

"So then the ski lifts get built," said the leader.

"Exactly. The southwest slope of the South Queen has the longest potential run in the state. They'll be helicopter skiing right up to the day the lifts and lodge are completed."

Arnie was not listening anymore. He had decided earlier that the ranger had forgotten about the ski lifts. His thoughts were on the gorp in his pack. His pack was in the sun, and the chocolate chips had probably collected at the bottom of the bag in a molten brown syrup.

"From the lodge they will groom a ten-foot-wide trail for the rugged sort who cross-country ski. This very cabin will likely serve as a warming hut at the end of it. There by the door will be a telephone and a pop machine. In that corner, video games."

Arnie heard these magic words. "All right!" he said.

"Skiers will use the trail in the mornings, and snowmobiles in the afternoons. When the snow melts, hikers and motorcycles will trade off in the same manner. But then you will be able to drive directly to the hut, the summer head-quarters for the School of Western Alpinism Guide Service. For eighty dollars SWAGS will lead you through the pipelines to a summit conquest, and then back to the park-ing lot in time for a getaway to the restaurant of your choice."

"Yum, pizza!" said one girl.

The leader was wondering if he could get a job with the new guide service. The pay sounded excellent. "What else will happen up here?" he asked.

"Well," said the ranger, "all the pipeline roads will provide good timber access too—that goes without saying. But once the boundary adjustments are made, yet another dream will be fulfilled. The deepest canyon beyond the South Queen—Amoenas Gorge—will become the site of a pic-turesque reservoir. The blessing will be complete: The wilder-ness shall become a pool of water."

"Can we water-ski up here then?" asked one girl. Without waiting for an answer, she turned to her friend. "I got up on one ski last week," she confided. "That's the first thing we'll do when we get back—go water skiing."

"After we go get pizza, you mean," said the other girl.

"That's for me!" crowed Arnie. "A sixteen-incher! Double cheese and onions and olives and sausage and pepperoni and Canadian bacon and pineapple and green peppers and toma-toes and mushroom and anchovies and . . ."

"*You* like anchovies?" The two girls were incredulous.

"Don't you?" said Arnie, equal in his unbelief. Then he appealed to the badge of authority: "Do you like anchovies?"

"Sometimes," said the ranger. She smiled.

Lunch was over, and the lecture with it. "Thank you," said everyone. "Thank you for the huckleberries."

"My pleasure," said the ranger. "Come again."

As the group filed out to their sun-warmed packs, the leader imagined what it would be like to steal a kiss in the shadow of the doorway.

15

THE SILVER BOX WAS ringing, and William's head sang like a clapper in a bell. Grace could hear the ringing too from the more aesthetic distance of six feet farther down the shaft. Here, wedged upright in a snarl of rope, she was much more attentive to William's creepers resting on her shoulders. Each blow on the box seemed to pound his spikes down deep into her flesh, bruising the darkness.

Still she did not speak, she did not squirm—did nothing to uncharm the shield and bring down ruin on their heads. So might meadow mice quietly crouch in the shadow of a hawk. Eventually the shadow passes, and so at last did the clamor overhead. The blows stopped, the din faded, a faint and far-away curse spun aloft. Then silence rolled down.

Grace listened to the air pour in at her lips. She waited for her eyes to adjust to the dark—for the wall, the rope, her hand to appear. But wait as she would, her eyes beheld nothing at all. She could not call it total darkness, for there was nothing total about it—it was not sum, but lack. It was only dark because the light was missing. The light did not come, and her eyes could not illumine the darkness. They were not the lamp of the body after all.

William meanwhile quietly lifted his feet from her shoulders. That felt worse. Now she was alone.

"William?" she whispered. "You still there?"

"I think so," he said. His voice echoed softly.

"She's gone, isn't she?"

"I think so," he repeated.

"When you lifted your feet up, I thought you'd left or something. Let's stay together, all right?"

"Good idea," he said.

"You sure you're okay, William? You don't sound so good."

"Just fine," he whispered.

"I can't see anything, can you?"

"Nope."

"Think you could open the lid and peek out? Get some light in here anyway?"

"Sure," said William, and he lifted up his hand. Then he brought it back. "What if they're waiting for us?"

This was a thought.

"Quiet!" she hissed. "Don't talk so loud then." She paused. "You think we should go down?"

"Okay."

"Don't say that! Say yes or no. You think this goes any-where?"

"Yes."

"Where?"

"Down, most likely."

She breathed disgust. "Do we have a light or anything?"

"Candles," said William. That meant finding their packs, which lay somewhere below them.

"I'll look," said Grace, which obviously she couldn't. She stretched out her foot as if testing the water in a pool. It touched one, two more steps, but no packs.

"William, why don't you go first? Would you? Just for a bit? Until we find our packs?"

"No room," he said.

She pressed the walls around her. A coffin would have been more spacious.

"Okay," she conceded. "I'll go first. But stay behind me, all right? Hang on to the rope or something so you don't lose me."

"Sure," he said.

She slid down one full step, then hesitated. "William?"

"Yes."

"Are you scared? I mean really. Tell me the truth."

Serious Climber though he was, William told the truth. "I'm terrified," he said.

"Good, me too. Let's be scared together, okay? It'll be nicer that way. When I was little, you know, my uncle would read me stories. Sometimes there were parts that got me frightened, and I'd cry. Then he would put down the book and hold me close, and I'd look up and see his eyes, and he'd say, 'I get scared too, niece.' It hardly seemed possible—that he could be scared—but it always made me feel better."

She paused. "William?"

"Yes?"

"I wish I could see your eyes right now."

He was flattered.

"Did you know Uncle Garth very well?" she asked.

"Not very well," he replied.

She thought this over. It seemed a bit odd. "Why do you suppose he picked you then? I mean, if he hardly knew you."

"Good question," he said.

Her thoughts began to take her where she did not wish to go. "Don't you think this whole thing is a little bizarre, William? I mean, sometimes I feel like everything's under control, and that my uncle has it all planned out somehow. But mostly I feel like everything happens by the foggiest luck. Like, things turn out, but just barely. Makes you think twice before climbing down a dark tunnel to meet who knows what—the Lava Beast, maybe?" She shuddered. All of a sudden it seemed so absurd.

"You know what my problem is?" she whined. "My problem is that I'm not very brave. I'm not, and I don't see the point of being here. Why we're supposed to go to all this trouble for the sake of a few marmots is beyond me, for heaven's sake. I didn't ask to come—this isn't the trip I signed up for, you know. Sometimes I wonder if he thinks this is some kind of a joke, playing around with us like this. I wonder if he is amused, seriously. I do. I wonder if right now—"

And right then, cutting her off, a peal of laughter sprang from above. William and Grace went utterly limp.

"Ah, Grace," came the voice. "You see the humor of it now! Your dear uncle couldn't go away unnoticed. He had to leave his little posthumous comedy." The voice trailed off into laughter again, and Grace began to whimper.

"Surprised to hear me, dear? It's only fair that if you hide under my bed, I hide next to your bedtime storybook. Did you read pleasant tales? Or did they frighten you, dear—make you cry? Let me comfort you with my eyes then.

"And William. Brave Sir Terrified William, defender and champion of marmots in distress. Such wisdom in your courage! Such discretion in your valor! Have you found your rusty ax yet, William? Do you think it lies under the mountain? What a pity it is not there.

"But you well know what is there, William. You know what lies in wait below. There's still time. Think on it, William. Show yourself wise. Open the shield while yet you can and come back out from your grave to the living. I have flung my dagger far away in the snow. Open the shield, William, and we shall make peace together. I that am above know how to be gracious; he that is below knows only to devour. Choose, William. Choose, then."

William stood quietly. His hand stung deep where she had slashed it. He did not feel like talking.

"Shy, William?"

He didn't answer.

She heaved a piteous sigh. "Have it your way then," she said. "And never pretend I did not try to help you.

"But, Grace, tell me, dear, why did you desert your young friend Lance? He's so lonely without you now. A pity too he shall never see you more. Unless, of course, you care to come with me. Then I could send you all back to your homes just as we'd planned, remember? This whole foolish business would all be over like a dream gone by."

She paused, but Grace did not respond.

"Won't you come, Grace? Do you really wish harm upon your friends? And upon yourself too? Or perhaps you are planning to desert William as well, somewhere deep in the bowels of the mountain when convenience offers."

Grace spoke before she knew it. "You deserted my uncle," she said flatly.

"Your uncle was a fool!" shouted Lady Lira. "And so are you both!"

In that instant Grace knew her uncle was not a fool.

"Farewell then," announced the woman. "The light of day bids you farewell."

The shield overhead rang out once more. This time Grace did not stay to listen. She launched her body down the shaft, creepers skating over the steps, striking out sparks like newborn stars. It was not safe, but it was not dull either. She stopped on a stair that was comfortably wide, with her feet punched into the soft underbelly of a packsack.

She turned around. "Come on!" she whispered.

She heard him slowly scrape to her side. There was room for both of them on the stair, and that felt good.

Once settled, William leaned forward and groped through the pack with his unhurt hand. On the bottom (of course) was a flint, a lantern, a fistful of candles—Colin's doing. He put all the candles but one in his pocket and readied the one to light.

The flint struck, the wick caught, the candle burned in a bloody mitten. He placed it in the lantern, and checkered holes of light and shadow sprayed the lava walls. The tunnel was lit.

There was room to stand up. They could see that now. And they could see a stairway curving downwards, first to Grace's tumbled pack, and then to her fallen ax, and last to a pair of marmot eyes, shining like planets on the edge of twilight. Grace looked at William's ashen face and then at his mitten, all in tatters.

"How did you do that?" she asked. She made him put the lantern down, and then held his wrist and peeled away the blood-soaked wool. The back of his hand was grisly to see.

"Does it hurt?"

He nodded.

She bound it with a handkerchief and told him to relax. He sank back placidly. Then she unstrapped his creepers, her creepers, and stowed them away. The rope she gathered in a snaky ball and stuffed it in her pack. The bread was in William's. She gave him some, but he ate very little. Grace ate much, and the marmot with her. She found a skin of water and drank it half down. William said he was not thirsty. So she put it away and fastened their packs. In theory, they were ready.

"William?"

"Uh huh."

"Do you think she was telling the truth about the Lava Beast?" She looked down the stairs. "You think he's waiting for us?"

"Probably," he said. His voice was utterly complacent.

She shook him by the shoulders. "What's the matter with you?"

"I'm fine," he said.

"You are not fine. Listen!" She grabbed his collar. "I'm

going down these stairs—all right?—and you're going with me. If we find a way out, we find a way out. That's all we can do." She remembered something the red-bearded leader had told them. "Buck up! Do your damnedest! Okay, William?" She looked him bang in the eye.

"Yes," he replied.

How far they descended she could not tell. The steps curled down, relentlessly left, and the ragged ceiling slipped by. Grace tried to count the steps at first, but always her mind would steal away to the tapping of their axes—tapping, tapping, tapping on the stone in still small echoes.

The marmot flirted in shadows ahead. He slipped beyond the lantern light, a vanished mirage, and softly reappeared. Then he waited, whiskers alert, watching them come—gone when they got there. It was nice to believe he knew where he was going.

Because they didn't. By the time their candle had burned very low, it seemed to Grace they had dropped too far—farther than they had climbed in the dawn. Her knees had begun to grate inside, as if pieces of lava were scouring the joints. It was warmer now. She was thirsty too. She wanted to stop.

She noticed then that the marmot himself had come to a halt. He was standing up on his hind feet and squinting back at the lantern. Beyond him the lantern light skipped and flashed. She drew up beside him and saw what it was—a black spread of water. The stairway ended just at the shore, and the walls flung apart in a half-submerged cavern.

She stooped, laid her ax aside, and gently combed the water. It was warm. She touched her fingers to her tongue. And it was wretched. She tried to spit the taste away.

William meanwhile sank down wearily on the steps. His eyes were vacant. Grace saw a twig that was caught in his hair and teased it out like a fretful mother. She carelessly tossed the twig in the water, and there it shone like a golden bough. Then it was gone, swept from sight.

"There's a current to it," she said aloud.

"A current to it, to it," her voice echoed back.

This gave her ideas. She lifted high the lantern and peered across the cavern. There in the shadows she saw what she was looking for—stairsteps climbing out of the water. There was another side. Perhaps the river could be forded.

She seized her ax and plunged it in. The end of the shaft struck one submerged step, then another. She sank it to the hilt on a third. Then dropping to her knees, she skated it out as far as she could reach—there did not seem to be a fourth step.

"I think we can wade it," she reported. William looked steadily at the water and said nothing. Grace did not see much use in consulting him. She stripped off their sweaters and stuffed them tightly in both packs, leaving her own pack partway open.

"You ride in here," she said to the marmot. She scooped him up and settled him inside. His head and forepaws poked out the top. Then she hoisted the pack to her shoulders, which took some straining. She felt the marmot's wet nose on the back of her neck.

William went through the motions of putting on his own pack. "Go steady," Grace told him. "Keep your hand on my waist."

They stood on the shore then—the mother, the marmot, the maimed—ready to test the waters. Carefully holding the lantern aloft, Grace splashed onto the first submerged stair. That was easy. The second stair was knee-deep, and it filled her boots with a thick warm flood. The marmot began to clutch her neck, and William gripped her waist. Still, it was trivial. But the third stair gave the current a voice. It called out softly from her thighs, insisting she turn her steps. She gathered her strength, edged out farther, inched her way against the swell. Another stair would sink her too deep. But the going was level—there were no more stairs. With dripping sleeve she plunged her ax to the left, to the right. She found no bottom. A drowned causeway, narrow as their hopes, was all that parted the waters.

"Stay close," she said to William. He stood half-submerged in the wake of her shadow, the shadow of himself.

Grace moved very slowly—one foot, the ax, the other foot, the ax again. It was hard to keep the narrow way. The water moaned around her thighs, pushing her where she dared not step. Before very long she grew weary of denying it, tired of bracing all her body. How easy, how desirable, to swerve, to sigh, and then to yield. She almost wished it.

So it was that the first stair caught her by surprise. When you are contemplating failure, success is a bizarre intrusion. She mounted out of the river's grasp, shedding the tips of its watery fingers. Two more steps and the river was gone, and her knickers hung wet on her thighs. William's hand still touched her waist. It was trembling.

"How are you doing?" asked Grace.

"Fine," said William. He shrugged off his pack, and it nearly rolled into the water.

"How about you?" she said to the marmot. As if to say that he was fine too, the marmot leapt out from the top of her pack and wandered into the shadows. She held up the lantern to watch him go. The way ahead looked smooth and stairless, but it was dim now, and she couldn't see far. The lantern was flickering badly.

"Got another candle?" she asked. He did. She replaced the stub in the lantern box and set the lantern aside.

Her feet were swimming in private ponds, and so were William's. She sat him down and plucked off his boots and poured libations to the river. She wrung his socks out one by one, and then dried his feet with the sweater from her pack. On the knuckles of his toes were a few wisps of hair.

She had scarcely put William together again when down the tunnel the marmot whistled—shrill urgency that seemed to echo from far away. But even as they turned to look, the marmot was upon them. And he did not stop. He careened from the dark like a rabbit pursued, shot between them, glanced off the lantern, gathered his paws for the final leap, and hurled himself into the river. The lantern tumbled after him and smacked the water in a deep dark hiss. Then all was black.

William and Grace sat very still. They were quite confused. But then they felt it—both at once. The air grew heavy, close, and hot. They tasted acrid smoke. The very floor grew warm beneath them. It was silent, it was dark, but it was coming, and they knew its name.

William groaned, forlorn and forsaken. His hand and even his chest ached horribly. The darkness thickened. It pierced his very heart.

Grace felt trapped and pressed and stifled—the way it had been beneath the bed while Lady Lira chanted. The same presence was closing now, like slow-moving magma, this time unmediated by mirrors and words and woven symbols. It came slowly, surely, for her alone: the thing itself. The wicked weight was more than she could bear.

It was up to Grace. She planted her ax like a pillar of stone and slowly began to rise. Slowly she rose, as if in a dream, as if she were crushed by a murderous burden. She reached for William, caught his arm, pressed his wounded hand. At first he would not move. But she gripped his wound till it bled once more and felt him give.

They would have to try. She turned and splashed in heavily: one step, two. The third step seemed to be farther down than it was before—much farther down. When the water closed over their heads, she still had not found it.

16

SHE LET GO OF her ax first. Then somewhere inside the warm womb of the current, Grace let go of William's hand. Was it instinct? Ah, but she knew the quality of her own instincts. Lady Lira had been right about her. She was merely a deserter. Now she had proven it clear to the end. Even as her breath grew short, she groped for him in the watery dark. But William was gone.

And then her breath grew very short. Groping still, her hands found the surface and brought it to her mouth. She gulped the darkness—three full breaths—and sank back into the river.

She began to wish things. She wished she had not stopped writing to her uncle. She wished she had not left Lance with Lady Lira. She even wished she had not run away from the red-bearded leader. She pondered her wishes under the water, and warm sorrow bathed her soul. Then, bit by bit, the memory of her sorrows ebbed away.

She mechanically reached for the surface again, and this time did not find it. She panicked, kicked upwards, knifed gasping into air. Unaccountably, the air she inhaled was no longer dark. She could see her hands in a shadowy light. The light was dim, like the first gray of dawn, just enough to hope by. So she worked her arms to stay afloat to see what she could see. Before very long her shoulders were aching. She wanted to rest, to sink once more. But that would be the third time.

Meanwhile, the light grew and her hopes with it. Walls and ceiling reappeared, slipped by. Then ahead, the water began to glint and flash as rivers do in the city at night. The pulse of the stream began to languish. It washed her into the glinting water and swept her round a bend. All at once she saw before her an open portal, radiant with a misty light. The light was not like that of the sun—it was harsh like the glare of a fire. Grace wafted through the portal like a freshly fallen leaf. She gently whirled in a vanishing eddy, and then the current was gone. Her feet touched bottom. Her body came to rest.

Where was she? Grace stood in the midst of a vast steaming lake in a cavern so tall she could not see the roof. All about her, just as in Lady Lira's mansion, torches were burning in brackets on the walls, spaced like angels around the shore. The walls of the cavern were far apart, and some of the torches she could not see because of the steam on the water. It swirled about her like morning fog, strangely lit by tongues of fire. All was eerily quiet here save lapping waves and sputtering flames.

Grace stood brooding in the waters, immersed except for her head and shoulders. She listened to the emptiness and found that because there was nothing to hear, she listened all the harder. And then she did hear something—a still small splashing that filled the void. Out of the mists came a lone little creature, paddling towards her like a beaver out of practice. Like a beaver, it held a stick in its teeth as it swam. Before it reached her, she knew him well—it was her marmot. In his jaws was her once-lost ice ax.

She took the ice ax from his mouth and touched his sagging whiskers. "Welcome back, little marmot," she said. She gathered him up, and he climbed to her shoulder. There he curled around her neck—a dripping marmot stole.

Now they were two. She felt his heart beating on the back of her neck and bent her cheek to his. The silence returned, but was not as empty as before. And yet, it was empty still. They needed a third.

When the marmot had caught his marmot breath, Grace turned and asked him, "What should we do?" Immediately, the marmot stood up on the top of her shoulder—as if only now he had just remembered what he never should have forgotten. Then without a word of explanation, he dove into the water and swam away.

"Where are you going?" Grace shouted. This was desertion.

The marmot disappeared in a white cloud of mist, and Grace lunged after him. "Wait up!" she called. Though he swam much faster than Grace could wade, she pressed her thighs against the water and followed in his wake. She guided herself by the sound of his splashing, and at last it stopped beneath a torch on the steam-wrapped shore ahead. She saw him there through the clouds.

And she also saw, as she forced her way, a man that stood in the water beside him. His back was slumped against the wall. His face hung down, shadowed by the torchlight. It had to be William.

Grace plunged to his side and held up his head—and William it was not. For a moment she gaped, adjusting disbelief. Then she kissed him, her own Lance Q. It was a long kiss, a fervent one. He slowly opened his weary eyes and fixed her with a faint smile. "About time," he murmured, and he kissed her in return. The marmot paddling at their side had never witnessed anything quite so marvelous.

After more greetings of this sort, Grace stepped back to better appraise him. At once she noticed a thick iron chain that hung from the wall and vanished in the water. "Are you connected to that thing?" she asked.

He was. Lance raised his arms from the water and displayed his shackled wrists. They were bound together in one iron cuff attached to the iron chain. He yanked it a little to prove that it held.

"Not good," said Grace. She grabbed the chain and pulled it herself. It was stuck fast in the wall. But she had an idea in hand—her ax.

"Stand back," she told the marmot. The marmot, however, had disappeared again—which was just as well since there was nothing for him to stand back on. Grace heaved the ice ax over her head, and with both her hands she brought it smashing against the rock where the chain was fixed. She did not expect much, and not much happened. The adze went glancing off the chain, shot towards Lance, and neatly grazed his lips.

"Hey, watch it," he said.

"Sorry," said Grace. She took a firmer grip this time and gathered up her faith. The second blow struck square and solid, where it was meant, and the rock crumbled out from the roots of the chain. But the chain still held. Now, however, she believed it could be broken. One more time she reared the ax and swung it with mind and heart and strength. The dolorous stroke hit hard, hit home, and the chain sprang free from the rock. That was the least of it. The entire wall came tumbling down in huge cracked chunks that splashed around them, leaving a hole at the waterline that gaped like an open door.

Lance and Grace both gaped in return.

"Some ice pick you got," said Lance.

"It's not mine," said Grace. "I'm borrowing it."

They looked inside the broken wall. It seemed quite hollow. How far it went they couldn't tell. Grace climbed out of

jelly-belly soft

the water first, and then pulled Lance up. He sat on the edge, feet in the water, clasping his fettered hands. They were jelly-soft and wrinkled from the wet. Meanwhile Grace stood up on tiptoe and plucked the torch from the wall above them. She brought it down and thrust it in; their recess came to light. And it was more than a recess. They were poised on the verge of a prickly passage, rough with lava spikes. It was the sort of tunnel that Grace had seen before.

"Any other ways out of here?" she asked.

Lance shook his head. "Not for us," he replied. His voice wavered. He looked out over the rising steam and then looked back at Grace. "The water goes out through a tunnel to the bog," he said. "We saw the end of the tunnel on our way to her house that first time, remember? Anyway, that's how I was brought in here. On the other side of the lake is a landing—she took me there first with all the marmots we caught." He shut his eyes and swallowed. "I wish I could forget," he whispered. "Let's go," he pleaded. "Please, let's go." Very quietly, Lance began to cry.

Grace looked down at the weeping boy and softly stroked his hair. She was all for going too—she just wished there were more of them to go.

And then there were more of them—too many more. From far across the lake she heard a terribly familiar voice.

"Stop the barge," it said. "Listen."

"What?" said another.

Why? thought Grace. She crouched on the brink and peered through the fog. Something silent slipped their way. But it wasn't a barge. It was her very own marmot, sleek as an otter, making his return. And that wasn't all. For behind the marmot came William himself, lumbering towards them with ice ax in hand. His hair was plastered on his brow, and his cheeks were wet and pale. He looked to Grace with the dazed expression of one whose mind is changed.

And then he was with her, raising himself from the waters of the lake, and the marmot with him, both man and marmot trying not to make a sound—which is easier for a marmot. The bandage was gone from William's hand; the gaps in his flesh lay fully exposed.

Grace pressed his fingers and put her mouth to his ear. "I'm sorry," she whispered. "I let go."

He in turn brought his lips to her ear. "I let go too," he told her.

Then William turned his eyes to Lance. He knelt beside him and touched his hands. They were still firmly anchored by the chain in the water. The boy was free but not free, loose but unable to escape. Even if they could lift the chain, it was bound to make much noise.

William inspected all sides of the fetters, running his fingers over the iron as if he were fondling an ax. He found underneath what he had learned to look for—a keyhole. He hoped he had the key to match. He drew it from his pocket and set it in the lock.

But the key would not turn.

There was one thing to do then. He looked at Lance. "Lay your hands on the ledge," he told him. "Close your eyes."

The boy obeyed.

"Hold the chain steady," he told Grace.

She did.

He took careful aim. He would have to split the manacles just between the wrists. The adze sang downward. The iron sounded, pealed like a bell. And the fetters cracked and fell asunder, cloven like firewood.

Lance opened his eyes. There was blood on his hands. Grace meanwhile had kept her hold on the loosened chain. Now she lowered it into the water and let go.

Then came the voice. "James?" it echoed. "It's time we checked on the sniveling boy."

Presumably that's what she did, but the three and the one slipped far away, and no one stayed to greet her.

17

A SNAP, A CRUMBLING opened her eyes, and firelight churned on the rafters. Grace lay dry and deep in her blankets. They scratched her a little, but she did not mind. She had no idea where she was, and she did not mind that either. Two more sleepers, swaddled in wool, were curled against her on either side, and that was enough.

She stretched her arms and brushed her fingers over a wooden floor. It was rough to the touch but soft on her back—as if she were lying on boughs of fir and not on planks of wood. Across the floor was a dark stone wall with a latticed window halfway up it. The window shuddered faintly. Strange as it seemed, snowflakes whirled thickly by, tapping on the glass. The light from the window was gray like winter dusk.

Grace turned from the storm and looked again at the roof beams in the firelight. She watched them for a long time. Then she half rose up to see the fire itself. It blazed at her feet, a generous fire in a fireplace made of round smooth stones improbably stacked like a house of eggs. Over the flames hung a blackened kettle, and stirring the kettle was a long wooden spoon, and holding the spoon was a fat old man who sat on a stool. His nose and cheeks shone red by the flames, and the top of his head shone too—for the man was as bald as his chimney stones. He was eyeing the kettle in a way that said he would love hot soup on a day like this.

Grace raised herself a little more and saw a steaming ball of fur rolled up inside the three stubby legs of the old man's stool. She vaguely recalled, like the memory of a dream, following the marmot through dark blowing snow, over piles of stones that were cold and wet—and soft somehow when she fell on them. She had followed him too down a rough lava passage and let him choose the way. Then the walls had turned to ice, glistening and black, devouring the light like greedy mirrors that gave back no reflection. Deep in the ice were buried faces, set in long anguish. Grace had glimpsed them, hurried on. Then the ice was white and turquoise, opaque swirls and mingled veins—bright in the torchlight. Waterfalls crashed in liquid columns; others held silence, frozen in place like pillars of salt. One chamber there was—too splendid to forget—where groves of crystals clung to the walls, radiant, delicate, soon dissolved in a single breath. Then had come darkness and driven snow, and this warm place that shut the storm away.

The old man caught her eye and winked. "And a good night's morning to you," he told her. "Can't say you didn't take the best way. Weather like this, why should a body get up? Not sure why I did, anyways. It'll come to me though." He stopped stirring the kettle and tasted the broth. "Ah, there it came, the *ratio surgendo*!"

Grace looked at him blankly.

"When you eat with the devil, you need a long spoon," he said, holding up his own. "You know why?"

"Why?" asked Grace.

"So if he doesn't mind his manners, you can smack him 'twixt the eyes, and that makes him cross-eyed, a good Christian demon. Then he'll be behaved and say your name before he eats."

"My name?" she said.

"Yes, he'll say Grace."

"When would he say *your* name?"

"Why, when he wants a second helping. 'Chambers!' he will say. 'Chambers, ho! Another pot of soup!' And so I get my chamber pot and soup him on the head and beat him out the door with my spoon!" The old man cackled with untold joy and rapped on the kettle like a drum.

"So your name is Chambers?"

"Sir Chambers, officially," he said, throwing back his shoulders. "It's Chambers to you though. We met last night or maybe this morning, but you were busy getting acquainted with those blankets. I was hoping you'd come, too—when I saw you yesterday."

Grace looked confused.

Chambers pointed his spoon behind him. "I keep an eye on things in the pond out back. Had a pretty close watch on you most of the time till it clouded up."

Grace still looked bewildered.

"Pond don't work when the sun's not out," he explained.

"You could see us?" Grace said. She remembered seeing others in the lid of the silver box on the mountain. How strange to think she might have been in someone else's picture.

"You was quite a show!" he cackled. "That's one mean woman. Always told your uncle he shouldn't put you up to this. But here you are, still in the flesh, so I guess he was right. Nothing recedes like regress, when you're headed that way."

He spooned out a bowl of soup and set it by her feet. She had to sit all the way up to reach it.

"You know my uncle?"

"He knows me," he said. "Haven't seen him lately though. I imagine you will soon—hard to say. Man pulls a stunt like that, and who knows where he's gone to—or his ax neither."

"How soon is soon?" said Grace. She was anxious. "When do we see him?"

"When it's finished," he said.

"Which is when?"

"It ain't finished till Lira's finished. You help your friend there find the ax. Then let him do the finishing."

"So why didn't Garth just give him the ax?"

"Because it's not just given. It's found too. You only know how to use the dern thing if you've looked a long time."

"Then I'm afraid I've botched it already," said Grace. "I was supposed to find directions in the summit book for us, but I couldn't read fast enough."

"Don't worry," he said. "You prob'ly found plenty good directions. Not all directions is east, west, north, and south."

He filled himself a bowl of soup and drank it off, coating his hoary mustache green. "I know a little about that book. It takes you back to get you forward. It opens above, and it closes below. You start at the middle and belong in the beginning and live in a blank at the end."

"That's right," she said. "The last pages were blank."

"You know my theory?" he asked. He leaned over and whispered it in her ear: "Invisible ink." Then he raised his eyebrows and nodded his chin in a most knowing fashion.

Grace decided on one more try. "Well, you know my theory?" she said in reply. "It's that I'm not even supposed to be here! Lance and I, we ditched our group—I don't know how long ago. But our leader has got to be worried by now, so we have to get back, see? It would be mean not to."

"Your leader?" said Chambers. "The ninny with the red beard? The one that lost the key to his nose, so he always has to pick it?"

She nodded solemnly.

"Ah, then don't worry, Grace. I told him you went home."

"A lie!" she hissed.

"Is it?"

"Of course. This is no place like home."

"Well, *semper lentus sed numquam certus* is what your uncle says—always slow but never sure."

"What does that have to do with anything?"

"I'm not sure. But if you want to get picky about it, there *is* no place like home."

"Like where?"

"Nowhere I know—that's the point. But take, say, this little room I know in the glacier cave up the hill. Maybe you've been to it on your way down here. The chamber's lined with these feathery crystals—no place prettier, no place more like home to me. What I'm never sure about is what to do once I get there. If I go inside, the crystals disappear when I step on 'em. Even breathing makes 'em collapse. But if I stay outside, I can't see 'em all. So usually I go inside. But I can never look it all in. Once I tried to take some crystals with me, but they melted in my hand. Once I carved my initials in the ice, but they melted too. Once I brought some blankets and slept there. Nearly froze. I woke up and thought to myself, *So I've slept here.* Then I chopped a bench in one wall where I could sit and look, and it didn't look any different from standing up. The next time, I brought some paper and tried to draw it all down, which I couldn't do, so I started writing instead. I wrote a whole list of words: *splendid, dazzling, radiant, delicate, exquisitious.* But the crystals hung in the cave, and the words pooled on the page—they weren't connected. So you see? I'm never quite sure how to make myself at home, even when I think I'm there."

Long before he had finished, Grace figured she was. She sank back in her blankets and resigned herself to many blank pages. "I'm not sure I follow," she murmured. "I guess I'm a little slow."

"It's the soup," replied Chambers. "Lentils make *lentus.*"

The window was dark now; the panes were still tapping as Grace fell asleep again.

Her eyes next opened in a shaft of sun. The fire had burned low, and the blankets beside her were broken empty like old cocoons. From an open door a quiet breeze came in and teased her hair. The air was fresh, and the walls and rafters were strangely bright, aglow with more than the morning sun.

She rose and went to the door—and saw why. All about her the land shone white beneath a warm blue sky. Whether the ground was barren or fertile, boulders or beargrass, she could not tell, for all was smothered with snow. There were no trees in sight. At her feet a pure white plain descended to a lake. Its waters, dark against dazzling shores, were ruffled by the breath of summer come again. Grace wondered if this were Chambers's pond. Above the lake rose a massive mountain that made it look like a pond indeed. The top of the peak was a broad smooth splendor; below it were cliff bands, reds and yellows, laced to perfection with new-fallen snow; then a sweep of glaciers that for all she knew came clear to the lake. It was a mountain that astonished. She guessed it to be the North Queen, and as she found out later, she was right.

Presently she saw the others. They were walking up from the lake to the cabin with pails of water in hand. Lance, she noticed, went shirtless. The veins in his arms were sharply etched from the strain and pull of the buckets. He looked up at Grace when they came near, but not for very long.

For breakfast they sat in the cabin door and said very little. It was too good a morning to spoil with speech. So the wind and the sun conversed alone—and talked the snow away. Drops fell down from the cabin eaves: few, many, many more, joining in a stream. The line of footsteps coming from the lake began to brim like springs. There were trickling sounds of water unseen, and then in hollows snow gave way to rivulets, noisily drenched in its own decay.

"Be all gone by afternoon," Chambers said. "Still summer, even though these hills get confused sometimes."

He looked out over his so-called pond, its surface broken by the warm full wind. Then he winked at Grace. "Don't work so good in the breeze neither," he said, "but I'll keep an eye on it for you. Maybe we can find where you're off to next."

Grace hoped to herself that the wind would hold. She did not feel like being off to anywhere that day.

She got her wish. Morning melted to afternoon, and they lolled beside the cabin, soaking in the sun, drying their clothes in the breeze. Chambers bandaged William's hand, applying to the wound three drops from a vial he had received from Lady Demaris—"practically neighbors," he said. Then he found three old canvas packs and set about sewing them up. Lance offered to help and stabbed his thumb with the needle six times. Grace volunteered to coach him then, and Chambers and William left them be. She knew little enough about sewing herself. Nevertheless, always slow but never sure, they sat on the doorstep and went to work.

At first they confined their conversation to the wonders of needle and thread. But by the time she had bled her own thumb dry, Grace found the courage to speak her mind and said she was sorry—she really was sorry—for running out on him just the other day at Lady Lira's house, and that even though she had sort of had to leave, it was the way she had felt that counted, and, well, she hoped he would forgive her, that's all, to which Lance replied that the fault was his, whereupon Grace reclaimed sole credit, whereupon Lance answered firmly that he alone deserved title to guilt, at which Grace insisted that she and she only was ever to blame, to which Lance said, "Shee-it."

At last they found it one bit funny and laughed together as old friends. When they had got their breath, they sat quite close and told their tales. Grace went first, and Lance believed her, every word; nothing seemed too awful or too wonderful anymore. Even so, Grace kept one part back, and it was not until Lance had had his turn, and the packs lay beside them against the cabin, long-since sewn up, that she confided her final secret—that, according to Lady Demaris, she was part-fairy. "She says that's why I see certain things."

"No kidding," said Lance. He edged away to regard her from a distance.

"Do you wish I weren't?" she asked, wishing she weren't and wishing she had kept it to herself.

"Sure—I mean, no—I mean . . ."

"You do! Admit it! You think I'm something totally bizarre!" she whined. "Listen to me, Lance. Most of me is normal. It's just a little bit that's different. It's like I still look the same and everything."

Grace knew she was floundering. She felt her face grow hot, her eyes grow moist. Without really knowing what she did, she jumped to her feet and ran away, out across the plain. The snow had all but melted.

Meanwhile, Chambers had taken William inside where they pored over wrinkled brown maps. "Don't know where you're going to," he said, "but at least you can get the lay of the land."

The maps showed features that our maps do not. Lava caverns and glacier caves and a maze of underground lakes and streams were marked in red and silver and blue. William whistled softly when Chambers traced the length of their subterranean journey. They had surfaced at the snout of the Mirror Glacier on the north flank of the Center Queen. Chambers's cabin lay just below on a high broad saddle that separated the Center Queen from the North.

Small green circles marked gathering places on meadow slopes or in forest glades. Here, explained Chambers, foot races and dances and song contests lasted far into midsummer evenings.

"Song contests?" William said, coloring slightly.

"The same," said Chambers. "Should've seen Colin go to it last time. Nobody better. But if you're still around by the next full moon, maybe you could challenge him."

"Maybe I could," said William.

Purple dots were scattered across the map below timberline. "Huckleberries," Chambers said, patting his rotund belly. "The very best patches. Getting to be the right season for 'em too."

Other spots on the map were marked with crossed ice axes.

"Mines?" asked William.

"No, sir. Battlegrounds. Historic sites. Places where the lackeys of the Lava Beast have had to reckon with the sorry likes of us."

William saw that the crossed axes stretched far westward into the lowland forests.

"Those are the oldest battles," said Chambers. "Lord knows, few of 'em won, and not enough of 'em fought. The ax doesn't show up all that often—and when it's around, it don't get used enough. We've lost a lot of ground."

He looked up at William, paused and spoke: "If the ax comes to you, William, let it do its work. It never strikes at the wrong time—that's what's good about it. Nobody gets hurt but what's supposed to get hurt."

William turned pale. He would rather no one at all got hurt, especially himself.

"We're part of a mighty tradition, William, that's got all the appearance of a lost cause. But one comes—maybe soon—who's said he'll destroy the destroyers of the earth. All we've lost he's already won. Don't ask me how. Just fight the good fight, man. That's all we're asked."

Outside the cabin the snow had vanished, and dark green heather stretched away on sodden slopes. The heather blossoms, tiny red and tiny white, tossed lightly in the breeze. The white ones hung down like puffed shoulders of linen blouses. That was Grace's impression, anyway, and where she knelt she could see them well. She was far from the cabin, out of breath, crying no longer. The snow-soaked heather had cooled her knees and soul.

In fact, all of her was cold. So she got up to walk, and not yet ready to face the others, she headed for the lake. As she walked, the west wind poured across her face, went streaming through her hair. She felt blown into place with the blank blue sky; she felt flung away with the heather. She could not see off the edge of this world to any forest below. Were it not for the lake and the North Queen above it, Grace would have had little sense of walking anywhere at all. The vast sameness, the windy expanse, seemed to mourn ~~its own~~ *its lack of* beauty. For a moment she was part of it.

She reached the darkly lapping lake and looked for her reflection. But the wind confused the waters. *Don't work so good in the breeze,* she thought. That was fine with her, wasn't it?

She saw a path in the heather along the bank. It beckoned her—that is the power of every path—and she followed. She walked it just to walk, or maybe to circle the shore, or maybe to keep warm. Sometimes the path crossed tiny streams that spilled into the lake. Each was only a step across, but she leapt them all with sailing grace, just for the joy of leaping.

She was halfway around when she met with a stream too wide to jump. It was boulder-strewn and milky blue, swift and noisy, cold to the touch. She was not about to wade it. This was far enough. She sat herself down on a rock by the lake shore, folding her arms around her knees to keep the breeze away. Across the lake and up the slope she could just see the cabin. It seemed very small from where she was, little more than a dot on a map. Above it domed the Center Queen, half-forgotten, less a place than a silvery dream. It was odd for a mountain to still exist once she had already been there.

While she was gazing, two small figures came down from the cabin—to fetch a pail of water, she supposed. Which two they were she could not tell. Then from over the western horizon, a single figure came gliding towards them. Was it the third of three, or another? Again she could not say. Those from the cabin reached the shore, and there the other joined them. Perhaps they were talking. But Grace heard only the wind.

When her eyes grew weary of prying from a distance, she fell to watching the lake at her feet. The surface was broken by gold-flecked ripples, and the waters were dark like buried ices—he could not see the bottom. In a way she was glad of it; she would shed no tear if her vision should perish. But in another way she desperately wanted to see what she could see.

And then she saw. The lake at her feet grew suddenly calm, and in the water—not reflected but real in its presence—the lovely face of a very young woman was gazing up at Grace. Her hair was golden, floating and falling, and twined with lavender shooting stars. Her eyes burned green, and her face and throat shone pure as the morning snow. The woman's arms were sapling smooth, and her breasts hovered deep in the icy waters like lilies drowned in crystal black. And fast in the grip of the woman's right hand, slowly rising toward the surface, was an ice ax.

It was unlike any ice ax Grace had seen. The head of the

ax shone brilliantly, like Sirius on a winter's eve. The wooden shaft was long and dark, and it shivered with curiously carved designs. Grace did not know which to watch—the woman's eyes or the rising ax. So she watched both, and neither.

The head of the ice ax closed with the surface, then broke the water like a silvery fish. The shaft slid upward, glistening wet, at crooked odds with its lower self till the woman's hand slipped out of the lake and held it fully aloft. The hand inclined the ax towards Grace. It hovered at arm's reach. As if in a trance, Grace put out her trembling hand and closed it around the head of the ax—thumb beneath the adze, fingers around the pick. She had it securely.

Or it had her. For in the moment she grasped it, her arm heaved forward almost out of the socket. It was like shaking hands with a man who decides to throw you to the ground. But the ax was different—it threw her in the lake. She was yanked from her rock with swiftest ease, and once she was in, the ice ax ripped itself from her hand.

Stunned by the cold, Grace thrashed about till her hands and knees struck bottom. She raised herself on her arms—and stopped. The unfathomed waters were lapping at her elbows. It was that deep, no deeper. There was no ax, no woman. Grace lunged ashore and stood up shaking, clutching herself. At her feet the water chopped and slapped, the way it had before.

She would have to think about this. First, however, she would have to dry out. So she lay down flat on the bare outcrop. There, out of the wind, the sun-warmed rock brought comfort. She wondered if William would have had the strength to wrest the ax away—that is, if it were really there, which it was not, in the end. In the beginning, though, the woman and the ax were more there than anything Grace had ever seen. The burning green eyes, the utter loveliness of the woman's face—Grace could not forget them. She would ask Chambers who it was.

Grace started back when she was warm enough to walk. Her clothes were still wet, but the afternoon was too far gone for the sun to dry them—they would have to be hung by the fire. Three figures remained on the far lake shore. They turned as Grace approached. She made out William by his up-and-down posture, Lance by his practiced slouch. The third was a woman in a plain gray smock. She guessed, she hoped, and then she knew: it was Lady Demaris. Grace waved her arms, and they all waved back. She could not help running the rest of the way.

"Lady Demaris!" she called. "What are you doing here?"

The woman caught Grace in her arms and kissed her on the forehead. "Dear Grace," she said, "I came for news of all of you. I was hoping Sir Chambers might have seen you in his tarn. But here you are, and this whole hour I have been marveling at your adventures."

In her hand she waved a graceful bouquet of purple asters. A basket of huckleberries, plump to bursting, lay at her feet. Lance's lips were already dyed a cyanotic blue.

"Have some, Grace," he said.

She ignored him without really meaning to.

"You look wet," said William. "Did you fall in the lake?"

"Not exactly," she answered. "I have to tell you—I think I saw the ax."

"The ax?" said William.

"The ath?" said Lance.

She felt the wind dry her lips as she told what she had seen. William looked nervous. "Then maybe we should go back," he stammered. "Maybe I could grab it." A new breeze gusted across the lake, and William's suggestion fell curiously flat on the waters.

"Lady Demaris," said Grace, "do you know who I saw? The woman had green eyes like yours—and like your sister's."

Lady Demaris smiled softly. "That is because she is our sister. You have seen the young and beautiful Stella. But you will not find her here, for though she lives in the waters of a lake, it is not this one."

She paused and sighed. "Years ago, before Lady Lira parted from us and when our father, Lord Linton, was still alive, we all four lived in the cottage by the Center Queen. No one delighted to climb with our father more than our sister Stella. From the first day she could wield an ax she followed his steps on every Queen. The North Queen, though, was much her favorite. When Stella grew older—and our father too old—she spent many a summer day alone, toiling up the glaciers of her best-loved mountain. On top is a great snowy crater—look, you can see the edge of it—always filled with a deep blue lake. The lake is said to be so pure that the stars themselves come down to drink. There on the crater rim, late into the summer night, Stella would linger and gaze upon the ice-bright stars drowned fast in the lake. All night she would watch until Venus alone lay bathing in the dawn.

"One morning, the dawn of deep midsummer, she did not come home from her all-night vigil. We all grew worried, our father especially, and I remember the rattle of his ax on the ice as we hurried up the mountain. All that we found was her small wooden ax plunged upright on the eastern rim."

"The one you gave me?" asked Grace.

Lady Demaris thought for a moment. "Yes," she said, "the very one."

Then she continued, "We did not know at first where Stella had gone. Only when our father took the key to the summit of the Center Queen, opened the shield, and read in the Book, did he find that Stella had given herself to the crater lake to live beneath its waters with the stars in the night. For all is recorded in the Book of the Queens, and some things are foretold. And each living person may only look once in the Book."

"The book I read?" asked Grace. "Why didn't you tell us this about the key and the book before?"

"Yes," said William, "you yourself said you didn't know what the key unlocked."

"Well!" said Lady Demaris. She laughed merrily and waved them off with her spray of asters. "You did not expect all the family secrets at once, did you?"

"Do you think we could find your sister on top of the North Queen?" asked William. "Would she give us the ax?"

"Perhaps," laughed Lady Demaris. And then, more seriously, "Very likely." And then in a grave voice, "Leave at dawn. No earlier, for the night is moonless and the dangers are many. But leave at dawn before Lady Lira gets wind of your presence. Her eyes are close, and her dagger is near."

"We will," promised William.

"Then farewell," said Lady Demaris abruptly. "I must return home before nightfall. My heart stays with you. May your steps be firm. Give my love to my dear sister, should you be able."

With that she gathered the basket of huckleberries under her arm and strode away down the lakeshore path. The wind had calmed; the lake was still. They watched her depart in the yellowing silence of late afternoon. Before she left the shore, Lady Demaris turned to bid a last good-bye, waving her aster bouquet. Grace waved in return and glanced at the woman's reflection in the water.

Her hand gripped William like jaws of a lizard. The face in the water was hard and cold. One arm cradled a snarling marmot; the other raised a dagger aloft. A puff of wind erased the image, and the woman turned, with her ~~flowers~~ and her ~~basket~~, and was gone.

violin

188

"What's the matter?" said William.

"That's not Lady Demaris," she whispered. "It's Lady Lira."

"Are you sure?" he asked. He fixed his eyes on the vanishing figure.

She was sure.

"Lance, did you see anything strange?" he said.

No answer came from behind them. They turned. Lance lay flat on his back in the heather, his head rolled listlessly to one side. The trickle from his lips shone brightest blue.

18

OUTSIDE THE CABIN THE heather burned orange; the sun was aground on the edge of the world, nearly interred in a wilderness sepulcher. Inside the cabin a small fire puttered against the shadows. Lance lay deathly still by the hearth. The others crouched beside him.

"One more huckleberry," Chambers said, "and he'd a been dead for the rest of his life. What a hazard that woman is." He shook his head.

"So he'll make it?" asked William.

"Let's hope so," he answered. "*Numquam certus*."

Grace looked on Lance as if her eyes could wake what slept there. "He's so pale—he's hardly breathing," she said. "There's nothing we can do?"

"Not here," said Chambers. "Up yonder, maybe." He nodded towards the rose-flushed peak in the window.

"Up there?" she said. "But that was *her* idea. That's right where she wants us. Besides, we can't believe her story, can we? I mean, why would she tell us the truth?"

"Because she had nothing to gain by lying," said Chambers. "I could've set you straight on Stella. It would only have exposed her to tell another tale. When you disguise yourself as an honest woman, honesty is part of the disguise."

"Then how did she know about the key and the book when Lady Demaris didn't?" asked William.

"She knew by cheating on her father," said Chambers. He sat down thoughtfully on the hearth. "When Lord Linton left on his last climb of the Center Queen, he strictly charged his daughters not to follow him. Lady Demaris stayed at home, but Lady Lira secretly stole to the edge of the summit and saw him read in the Book. He was weeping as he read, and looking up, he saw her and wept the harder. Ashamed, Lady Lira came to him. 'It is not for Stella that I weep,' he told her, 'but for you, my daughter.' Having said this, his heart broke, and he died. Lady Lira reached for the Book, but a great wind blew it shut, and the shield closed over it. She reached for the key in the lock, but it vanished in her grasp. All this I saw in my pond."

"And you have seen Stella too?" said Grace.

"Yes," said Chambers, "but only on the morning she failed to return. That's how her sisters know what became of her. I'm the one that told 'em. But today, Lady Lira couldn't stay quiet about the Book. It's on her mind constantly. The Lava Beast, see, wants it destroyed."

William took the key from his pocket and held it up in the firelight. "So she wants this too," he said. He offered the key to Chambers. "Maybe you should keep it."

"Nope," said Chambers, "you'll still be needing it. When you reach the lake atop the North Queen, you must give it to Stella. It's your key to the ax."

"But won't Lady Lira be up there waiting for us?" said Grace.

"Not if you leave tonight," he said. "No reason to wait till dawn—it's never really dark on a glacier. She only wanted to delay you. Lady Lira has a nightly appointment to keep. The Lava Beast never likes to miss a meal. But she'll be back in the morning, first thing. You know how fast she is on her feet."

Grace felt an appalling hollowness inside. The firelight on the four stone walls seemed so much better than another icy peak in outer darkness. "Wouldn't it be safer to stay here?" she said. "I mean . . ." Her voice trailed off.

Chambers looked her in the eye. "Lots safer," he replied.

Grace realized then that some things were like this. You didn't so much decide to do them as they decided to be done by you. It was as it had been when she had fallen in the underground river. Once in, she couldn't decide to swim upstream.

She reached down and stroked her marmot. His fur was already warmed by the fire. "I'll go if you go," she whispered.

They packed quickly; the window was already dark. Sir Chambers gave them a frayed rope and some rusty creepers, stiff woolen cloaks and mittens with holes. He filled their bellies with soup and their packs with provision and showed them to the door. They were ready that fast.

Grace stood outside shivering in the shady damp, not really listening as the two men plotted the route. She heard a few words like *hourglass, schrund, cornice,* but what she saw through the open door was Lance lying deathly pale by the fire. Then the door closed. They belonged to the stars.

William went first. The heather was uneven, and not yet adjusted to the subtlety of starlight, he stumbled in the dark. He knew the climb would take all night, and Grace did not. She was going to ask but saved her breath. Silence is swift, and it seemed to her that William was too. She hoped that she could keep the pace—and keep the peace, as well. She promised herself she would not get angry. As they passed through the night, a breeze still blew, and it brushed her lips like wings of a moth.

The lake slipped by, bristling with broken stars. Halfway around it they found and followed the wrinkled noise of the stream that Grace had seen in the day. It led their feet on spongy slopes, up, away, till heather disappeared. Moraines arose, darker than sky, and the stream sank into stones. They heard it sound beneath their feet, full of noise, bereft of sub-stance, and kept on following what they heard. By echo of the buried stream they wound a way through walls of rubble, grateful not to climb them.

Then moraines melted away; the hidden gush of the stream fell silent. Stones lay scattered, and under them, like a polished floor half-hidden by marbles, was hard and gleam-ing ice. Before them now rose the dim white veil of a glacier.

They stopped.

"Tired?" asked William.

"No," said Grace. Oddly enough, she was telling the truth.

William unpacked the rope and the creepers, and they put them on. When all was ready, he felt her knot twice over with his fingertips. Then he left, and she heard his ax click against stones on the ice. The sound was fading when the rope tugged hard. It nearly sent her sprawling. Not so fast! she almost called. But this time she wanted things to be different. She wanted to keep up, to weed the tiny grudge before it flourished in her heart.

So Grace doggedly went to it, stumbling at first, mutter-ing at times; but at length the glacier lost its stone cover, and her feet bit smoothly across the ice. The rope began to glide, a single canoe on glassy waters. And Chambers was right—it is never really dark on a glacier. Even without the light of the moon, their path was strangely luminous. It was especially bright where the ice was covered with skiffs of fresh snow. Up here it had not all melted.

Soon, however, the glacier was torn by a crisscross snarl of dark crevasses, none of them wide, but all of them unimag-inably deep (or so Grace imagined). Most she could stride across; a few she had to hop. But one small step for Grace was a leap of faith for the nerve-racked marmot, and before very long she stowed him away in the top of her pack.

Beyond this maze the steely ice gave way to old firn snow

that remained from winter. It steepened quickly and hid beneath a mantle of the snow freshly fallen. William kicked through the loose layer into the firn and made a ladder of steps for Grace. Her creepers found good purchase at first, but as the slope grew steeper, the steps grew smaller. Soon she stood on only her toes and hung her heels in space.

Because of the steepness, William had begun to chop the footholds with his ax. Grace waited beneath him in showers of crystals, more at leisure to glance about as each new step was made. The mountainside was high and airy. This made her grateful for the relative darkness; it muffled the distance to the glacier below and obliterated all else—all, that is, save a faint speck of light beneath her heels, hovering like an earthbound star. That, she knew, was the fire-lit window of Chambers's cabin. Should she slip, she might float like a feather to his comforting hearth.

Slowly, unsurely, William lengthened their ladder of steps. The night already seemed far gone. On left and on right the stars had begun to disappear. But it was not the dawn that erased the stars—it was cliffs of rock. The snow that they climbed was pinching down in a narrow funnel, buried from the sky. The walls of the funnel were tall enough to eat the heavens away. It was dark inside.

They were deep in this cleft when something whizzed by Grace's head—something swift, small, like a spring-crazed swallow. Then, gone before it came, something else dove past her ear.

"Quick!" she heard. "Up here."

She had no choice. The rope popped her up like a bucket on a windlass and pulled her under a balcony of snow. It was a sort of cave that she suddenly entered—an overhung crevasse, really. They stood inside on a small ice shelf. Outside, the air screamed softly.

"Steam vents up above," said William. He was matter-of-fact in his explanation. "They warm the snow, and that loosens the rocks. Once we get above this spot, the chute opens up. If we stay to the side, we'll miss the worst of it."

Just as he finished, an ugly volley raked the roof. Then it was silent, and the silence lasted for several minutes. Did he dare? William took a deep breath and edged outside. On cue, a single stone shot over his head. He ducked back in.

"This is serious," said Grace.

He looked at her, but could not really see her face in the dark.

"Aren't you scared?" she asked.

"Me?" he replied. The pronoun was alien to his person; it was as if he had specified someone else.

Another precarious calm descended. The longer it lasted, the more fragile it seemed. But they could not get past "seemed." The problem with fate was its unguessability. So William stopped guessing and peeked outside. It was still quiet.

He stood out from their shelter and strained his eyes for a way to get over the bergschrund. It belted the waist of their hourglass funnel, splitting the firn from wall to wall. Next to one wall, however, the gap was bridged by a sliver of snow. He carefully traversed to it, staying beneath the bergschrund lip. The bridge was nearly vertical and so slender that he feared to touch it. But there was no other way.

Before committing himself, he chopped two steps with delicate strokes. Nothing toppled. So he mounted the steps in the way that a cat hops up on broken glass. Then he chopped two more. And two more. The top of the bridge, he knew, would be the weakest. He reached it nimbly, poised himself for an uncertain moment, and drove his ice ax over the lip. He felt the shaft sink firm to the hilt. It was blessed assurance.

Grace watched him vanish over the brink, and she waited until the rope pulled taut. She was more ready than she knew.

With fear-born ease she crawled to the bridge, swam to the top, and flung herself gasping over the lip—gasping because of the furry paws that had her by the throat. It was splendidly done, and she knew it. From there she stumbled up easier ground to where William waited beside the wall, away from the center of the funnel. He was pulling the rope around his ax, which was plunged in the snow by his feet. When she reached his side, he dropped the rope and solemnly shook her mitten.

"Hard part's over," he said.

Grace smiled in the dark. They were climbers.

So they climbed on. The slope grew wider, the going more gentle—gentle enough for the marmot to walk on his own four feet. They veered away from the center of the bowl, whence sometimes drifted the whir and clatter of falling rocks—which minutes before could break their bones but now would never hurt them. Grace felt almost smug.

But without warning, her satisfaction wilted in a sulphurous cloud of steam. It hissed at them from vents in the rocks, noxious, defiling, odor most foul. It drilled their skulls like a vengeful dentist who will not let up, no, not even when you are squirming in the chair, and tears are raining down your cheeks. Grace squeezed her head between her hands; she marveled at the pain. It was not pleasant.

And it got worse. New gusts of wind redoubled the fumes, served them up in a cold force-feeding. She choked, she spat, she staggered about in dull, disjointed steps. Grace wanted to stop. She wanted to chop out her grave in the snow.

But gradually she found reason to breathe. For bit by bit, like fog in sun, the sulphur was washed from the air. As they climbed higher, the wind blew fresh, and they left the hissing steam vents behind. As an emblem of hope, they saw on their right a crescent moon, newly risen, and on either side the mountain began to curve away in silvered purity—not a concave curve, as in the sulphurous bowl they emerged from, but a perfect convex rounding. This was the final summit cone, higher by far than the sister Queens they dimly saw below them. Far to their right at the edge of the stars crept a faint glow—very faint—promising the dawn. Overhead the Dragon threatened, the Dippers poured out blessing.

The snowslope grew a little steeper, though not too steep for the marmot. They switchbacked up in angling symmetry, kicking, breathing, rising in rhythm. Grace felt as if she were climbing on another mountain, somehow separate from the one below shedding rocks and steam. This mountain floated, disembodied, unwilling to mingle its roots with earth. It seemed a place where the stars might dwell. She wanted to climb it world without end, to keep on moving and stay where she was and never reach the top.

So it was all too soon, to Grace's mind, when they crested the crater rim. Here the breeze blew strong in their faces. They stood on the edge of a vast snowy ring, a perfect circle. The summit was everywhere and nowhere, and for this reason the North Queen had never been dear to William's heart. It was one mountain that would not yield the desired feeling of conquest.

Grace stepped towards the inner brink, but William pulled her back. "There are cornices here on the south and the west," he explained. "It's not safe near the edge." Grace did not know what cornices were. They sounded quite sinister.

William led her around the crater to the opposite side—the northern edge—a quarter-mile distant. They swept the rim like the hand of a clock, and when the clock struck twelve, they shed their packs, knelt on the verge, and peered inside. Their eyes were watering in the wind, but still they saw. They saw virgin snowslopes drop away, cupped in starlit stasis. And when they looked to the bottom, they thought that they saw through a hole in the earth to the sky beneath—except the sky in the crater was so much purer, so much more abounding in the brightest of stars that it couldn't have been this world's sky at all. Grace told herself it was simply a lake. Her eyes knew better.

For a very long time they contemplated the crystal shores, the starry depths, and lost themselves in looking. The dawn began paling the eastern sky, but they did not know it.

William was first to look up. He could see Grace's face in the dawn's early light. It shone with its own morning glory.

"See anything?" he asked.

"Stars," she murmured.

He rose to his feet and suggested they go down.

"How?" said Grace. To her it looked steep.

By way of reply he mimed a way to descend steep snow—plunging the heels, locking the knees. She would go first, he said. That way he could stop her on the rope if she slid toward the water.

Grace had her doubts, but she got up anyhow. "Stay here," she told the marmot. And with that she tottered over the brink. Just one step took her out of the wind, into an amphitheater of calm. Nothing appeared save water below, sky above, snow between—a curious universe. For the first time she noticed the lip of the crater across the way. It was overhung, curled inwards like ocean surf. This, she guessed, was the shape of a cornice. As she descended, she saw it more clearly, outlined in the dawn.

Her heels sank firmly into the snow. To descend was more like floating than walking. She relaxed in the rhythm, forgot to fear, and soon drew up at the margin of the lake. Fewer stars shone overhead now; the sky was losing its night hue, and the lake was gaining a turquoise glow. The waters spread motionless at her feet.

By the time William joined her, she had stomped out a

platform big enough for both of them. William nested the rope in the snow. He didn't want it wet.

"See anything now?" he asked.

Grace looked everywhere. Her toes were growing cold on the platform. "Nothing," she said.

"So now what?"

Grace had an idea. "Remember what Chambers said about the key? About giving it to Stella? Maybe you should toss it in and let her know we're here."

William shrugged his shoulders. Why not? he seemed to say. And he bit off one mitten to search his pockets bare-handed. He drew out the key and held it aloft as one holds up a glass of wine. Then plunging his ax well out of the way, he hurled the key in a glittering arc. It met the lake with a comic *bluup*! Ring after ring rippled out from its sinking place. They watched the outer ring grow large, large as the lake itself,

> As when a stone is into water cast,
> One circle doth another circle make,
> Till the last circle touch the banke at last.

And at that very moment, the moment of touching, the crater shook with a sharp report that jolted them to their knees. Their little platform bobbed beneath them.

"We're floating!" cried William.

They were. Their platform had calved off into the lake. Now it was a snowberg, drifting from the bank. Grace's ax was planted beside them, but William's was not. It was not on shore either.

"No more ax," said William.

Grace said nothing. She trembled on her knees and did not move for fear their island would overturn. The water around them was swimming-pool blue, but it was not for swimming.

And so they wafted out from shore, rocking as in a cradle. By and by they came to rest at the center of the lake, marking the spot where the key had sunk. And there, quietly, not as bursting vision but as simple fact, the lovely face appeared once more, smiling up at Grace.

"She's here," whispered Grace.

William lurched to Grace's side, and the berg tipped hard. They tossed up and down like a tree in the wind and nearly fell in the water.

When the snowberg settled, he peered off the edge. "I don't see her," he said. "Did I scare her away?"

"No," replied Grace. "She's smiling again. I think you amuse her."

Grace saw the woman's hair luxuriate in the water. It swayed like tall, wild grass in autumn. A circlet on her brow shone not with flowers but with gems—or were they stars? But the eyes, the lips, the lovely breasts: it was the same woman once again.

> *And she is known to every star,*
> *And every wind that blows.*

The ancient ice ax rested in her right hand, its silver head burning like winter sun. It was slowly drifting towards the surface.

"Give me your hand," Grace whispered to William. She guided it out over the water, poising his fingers where the ax would emerge.

"When it comes up," she told him, "pull very hard."

"But I don't see it," William said.

Even as he spoke, the gleaming adze broke the surface, and his hand recoiled. The dripping head of the ax rose higher; the dark wood slid like a sapling from the earth.

Then—and William saw it—the strong slender hand pushed out of the water, raising the ax aloft in its grip.

"Take it," urged Grace.

William moved with glacial swiftness, which is to say, he did not perceptibly move at all. The arm of the woman inclined the ax till it hovered beside his bare and listless hand. A bead of sweat dripped off one fingertip.

"Take it," said Grace.

And then he did. He gripped the ax, and it was his. The woman's hand released the shaft and sank beneath the waters. Grace glimpsed her face for one last time before it disappeared beneath them. At once they started floating back to shore.

"She's pushing us, I think," said Grace.

William hardly noticed. He held the ax at arm's length, possessed by fear and holy disbelief. He looked on nothing else.

Suddenly the air was perplexed with song. Wordless notes, wildly sweet, swirled around them like water round an oar.

"Look!" called Grace. She pointed to the crater rim.

Shining round about its lip, spaced like the stars on Stella's brow, stood brilliant white figures, blazing in the dawn. One light only hung now in the sky, sole director of the song. No other stars remained aloft, unless—but no, they refused to think it—unless the singers on the summit were the stars themselves, come down with wetted fingers to cool the tongue of lowly earth, to grant one brief taste of the music of the spheres. Their harmony whirled like rising steam; it echoed through the crater like swiftly shooting stones; it lapped at their ears like quiet waters.

Once, a long time before, William's mother had awakened him deep in the night and led him by the hand out onto the lawn. The neighbors were standing on their lawns too, bathing their feet in the nighttime dew and looking up at the sky. William looked with them. The heavens were shivering the glory of green. They were rippling, frothing like pools of a waterfall. He saw the green sky part in two, heal together, die to itself once more. "The northern lights," his mother told him. Now, floating on a snowberg, dumbstruck again by a chorus of the skies, William remembered the northern lights and sobbed within himself. The music he heard was the music he had seen.

For Grace it was different. Her memory presented a line from a poem that her uncle had read aloud to her in his musty room at the top of the stairs:

Poore verdant foole! and now green Ice!

For a moment she could see her uncle—really see him. She sat in his scratchy lap once more as he read each word with slow, soft pleasure: "Poor verdant fool!" He looked at her as he said it. His eyes held the music that was hidden at the borders of the words. And now it was this same music, released by the song from the hinting lands of language, that pierced her through.

Before they were aware, the tiny barge moored itself to the bank, filling the gap from whence it came. It fit like a key. Grace and William stepped ashore as if in a dream, gazing upward at the shining ones. The faces burned too brightly to be seen, and William covered his eyes. But Grace was granted—what? a moment's glance? She remembered it so well afterwards that it seemed an hour's contemplation. She saw a glorious woman, and yet no woman, naked and yet fully clothed in a radiance that held every color, green above all—an emerald rainbow. Most astonishing, the woman was looking directly at Grace. Her gaze was not soft, like that of Stella's upturned face, but full of terrible benevolence. Grace looked away. It was a fearful thing to be singled out by unknown glory.

And in the instant that Grace averted her eyes, the song ceased. All was calm. They looked again, and the shining figures were no more. And yet, as William and Grace traced the empty rim above them, whitened by the rays of the risen sun, they were certain the song had not really ended, that it had continued and would continue. Just then they wanted nothing else than ears to hear the song once more. But they sensed it would be years before it came to them again. *Even so,* they thought, *come.*

They turned to each other and exhaled the wonder trapped in their lungs. For a bare moment their eyes met. Then William looked to his ax. He held it closer to his side now. He held it thoughtfully. Then, without a word, he trudged up the slope. Grace waited till all of the rope at her feet went snaking after him. Then she followed in his steps.

19

WAITING ON THE RIM was the flat white light of morning full come, more banal than brilliant. It was windless, almost warm. The marmot lay asleep on Grace's pack—dreaming, perhaps, of distant green meadows. But what fool would go about to expound this dream? Not Grace. Not William. They surveyed the bowl of late summer snow, the quaint but perfectly natural lake, and wondered if these were places of miracle after all. Where were they when the morning stars sang together?

They did not agree on what to do next. William was for retreating down the other side of the mountain. His instincts told him never to stay on a summit too long. Grace, however, thought they should wait for Lady Lira, who was sure to come. And what, William asked, would they do when she got there? "Heave-ho? Have at her? Chop away like she was a block of ice?"

Ill at ease, out of sorts, he traced the crater rim. All was blank; and then, all was not. A dark silhouette was emerging on the south, growing like a shadow. They had stayed too long.

"Look who's here," said William softly. And as Grace turned, a horrible scream rent the crater. Again it sounded, shuddering in the air. The marmot awoke. He bristled like a cat. Then the scream mingled with a whistling cacophony of many marmots, all gathered at the feet of the silhouetted woman. It was a battle cry they voiced, a lust-song for blood.

As before, the woman and the marmots divided to conquer. She stretched her arm rightward, pointed the way. Instantly, her marmots broke free and galloped the rim towards the rising sun. One marmot only remained at her side. For a moment she stood with her arm still raised. Then she wheeled, and the marmot with her, and began to circle west.

"Grace?" said William. He had untied his knot and was untying hers. "Grace? Take your ax and your marmot and hold off the pack of them if you can. I'll take care of Lady Lira." How easily he had said it. It amazed him.

"Sure," whispered Grace. "I can do it." Her throat was dry. She felt William pat her shoulder in a most awkward way. Beside her the marmot stood ramrod erect, eyes bright. "Well, let's go then," she told him. And off they ran.

By now the pack of hoary marmots was already close to the eastern rim. They swept along like the second hand of a clock keeping time in a mirror. Grace swept not so smoothly. What adrenalin she had was drained by the altitude. Her lungs burned, her creepers weighed like lead on her feet. Her marmot pranced like a windblown leaf, but Grace could only stumble.

The marmots came swinging around the bend, paws flying, mouths drooling, yellow eyes ablaze. Grace had once seen a painting of a cavalry charge—at Waterloo, she believed—in which horses and riders burst recklessly at her, and every face—even those of the horses—was terribly twisted and savage. If these marmots would pause, just for a moment, she could sketch a picture much like that one—or at least take a photograph. But the marmots did not pause. Grace braced herself for the full shock, ready to plow headlong into carnage. She even felt a flicker of bravery. But then she slipped.

She did not slip, really. The spikes on one foot merely snagged a bootlace on the other. All the same she fell down flat—and the ice ax flew from her hands. The airborne shaft, her one last hope, met the charging marmots with no real force. It struck none, but touched them all, harmlessly sliding across their backs like a mother's caress. Grace cringed in the snow and kicked her feet to disentangle her laces. Perforce she awaited nature red in tooth and claw.

They were upon her in an instant, tearing at her cheeks with soft wet noses, slashing her neck with leather-smooth paws. A dozen of them ravaged her spine in a tumbling circus. To a marmot, they were merciless in their affection. It was more than Grace could endure. She rolled to her side, and they swarmed into her arms, each one desperately wanting to be petted. And so she petted them, every one, stroking their heads and holding each in turn to her face. Beside them lay her fallen ax. She looked at it and wondered.

William, meanwhile, rushed apace to the western front. Lady Lira came striding on in her tireless, efficient way, smiling at him in cruel amusement. Her marmot was running to keep her pace. William ran too, like a lover to his own, and for no good reason. The air was too thin. He wheezed and watched his vision dissolve in gray dotty flashes.

When almost upon her, he slowed to recover and cast a glance across the crater. How was Grace faring? He squinted. Not well, he decided. She was down, motionless, buried in marmots. They swarmed her body like ravens at a cache. He stopped. A groan, a curse escaped his lips. He clutched the ax till his fingers trembled and dashed it in the snow. He was becoming something he never had been—utterly furious. William had been irritated most of his life, but nothing in all his computer-placid days had ever taught him fury.

Lady Lira had stopped. She was waiting for him, jauntily dangling the dagger from her hand, and James too, snarling at her side. Very deliberately, William walked to within ten paces and halted. He eyed them warily. Lady Lira wore a tight-fitting hood which hid all of her hair. Her dress was thick and black. William had seen the like in old photograph books. Women wore such dresses years ago for climbing mountains. William remembered how stern the women had looked in the photographs. Lady Lira looked more than stern. She looked scornful.

"Fool," she said. "You tasted no berries, but today you will feed on these blossoms." She held up her dagger as if it were part of an obscene gesture.

"Look there," she told him, pointing to the far rim. "Look how your Grace makes a meal for my marmots. Such a long climb makes them hungry. And of course, they themselves need to be fattened.

"Don't you feel sorry for her, William? Don't you feel sorry that you sent her to her end because you wanted to face Lady Lira alone? Send the pawns off to slaughter while kings and queens prove their prowess in single combat—a noble tradition, no?

"And have you now a magic ax from the dead hand of my drowned sister? Fancy, now. Ax or no, I think you do not even have the will to fight. Do you not fear me? Do I not see your hand tremble on the shaft? You have good cause to tremble, William. I shall soon cast your carcass to the lake below to join my sister in a watery grave. Here is my steel, William. Taste it, feed deeply."

She laughed out loud when her taunt was finished. William stood quietly.

"Have you nothing to say?" she asked.

"I—I never liked you," he replied lamely. "All the same, I never thought I'd try to hurt anyone." He contemplated this.

"But look what you've done!" he burst out. "Look what you've done to Lance with your poison! Look what you've done to Grace with your marmots! And the marmots—look what you've done to them for the sake of your filthy Lava Beast!"

He tore open his coat, tore open his shirt and exposed the white scars over his heart: "And look what he did to me!" Then he held up his scarred hand: "And look what you did." He spat at her feet.

"Lady Lira," he said, "whether or not this ax be magic, I suggest you look out for it."

He looked at the ax thoughtfully, surprised at his own vehemence. Then he murmured, "And would I gore such a woman as you? And gore such a woman? And gore such . . . ?" He was stammering to himself now—boast had turned into soliloquy.

When he realized he had finished, William stepped cautiously forward. Lady Lira's plan, he guessed, was to harry him with her marmot and wait for the time to step in with her dagger. Matched alone against his long-handled ax, she'd have less of a chance.

He was right about her tactics. James leapt forward and sank his teeth so quickly into William's knee that William only gaped. Too late he sawed the air with his foot—the marmot had flashed behind him. He twirled and sliced with a stroke of the adze, but James was gone again. And so it went. The wily marmot darted here, darted there, and William tangled limb with limb in trying to get in just one blow. All the while he kept half an eye on Lady Lira, which was half an eye too little. For in the midst of the dance, she reached in quickly from the side. One clean slash laid open his forearm. William howled. It was most unfair. The wound bled like a sickly fountain, dyeing the snow scarlet.

So William decided to forget about the marmot. He

turned and charged at the black-robed woman. She leapt back lightly to the rim, and then leaned forward with her dagger thrust toward him. It looked extraordinarily long. The marmot tore madly at the back of his thighs, leaping from the snow like salmon in white water. But William ignored him.

He realized he could wait no longer. With both his hands he heaved the ice ax over his head, poised it to bury the pick in her heart and be done with the bloody business. With all his might he swung the shaft. But he missed his aim, missed it so badly that he wondered if the ax had a mind of its own. For the ax struck nowhere near Lady Lira. Instead it gouged deep in the snow between them—so deep that it stuck fast. A sword in a stone could not be more fixed.

"Aha!" screamed Lady Lira. "What power in your ice ax now?" She reared back her dagger to deliver the death stroke while William struggled to retrieve his ax. Her arm drove forward. The blow had all but fallen when suddenly—*pfft!*—a hairline crack split the snow between them, shooting out from the buried ax. The rim released a muffled groan. And Lady Lira was gone. The entire cornice on which she stood had split away at William's feet. His very toes hung over the crater. The ax rested free in his hands.

He watched, amazed, as Lady Lira dropped away, riding the fallen cornice. The snow was intact, the woman on her feet, the dagger still aloft in her grip. But when the cornice hit the edge of the lake, it sent up a towering curtain of spray and broke in a thousand pieces. Lady Lira was jolted into the water. She screamed, she flailed, she tossed her tightly hooded head—which to William's addled imagination looked very much like a ripe black olive bobbing about in a crushed ice cocktail. Her dagger, of no use to her now, flew glittering from her hand. It splashed in the very center of the lake and sank from sight.

"James!" she cried. "Help me, you fool! James!"

"What?" said the marmot. He nervously crept to the broken edge and glowered down at the lake. Then, abruptly, he turned tail and sped away down the side of the mountain. And William never saw him again. Or maybe he did.

"Help me!" screeched Lady Lira. "Help! Please!"

William paid her no mind. He turned from the rim and began to stumble dizzily back around the crater. Maybe he could still help Grace. His arm left a wandering crimson line that followed in his tracks. The snow was growing dim and splotchy; it danced with pinprick flashes of light. The screaming woman in the lake below seemed far away, a remnant from a dream, a story told by a lost acquaintance.

He was nearly to Grace when the marmots suddenly left their prey and rampaged towards fresh meat. He staggered to a halt, set his feet, drew back his wavering ax to dispatch them. But he had not the strength. The marmots cruelly set upon him and felled him to the snow. Their noses nuzzled without mercy. Their whiskers savagely tickled his face. He closed his eyes and lay in darkness. He had fought the good fight.

After a time, a gentle hand lifted his head. "William, you all right?" said Grace.

He opened his eyes. Things were clearer—the world had less of dance and flash. The cold snow on his outstretched arm had begun to damp the bleeding.

"You aren't all eaten up, Grace?" He asked it like a little boy.

"Not at all," she said. "I think they like us."

The shrieking below had intensified. "For the love of my sisters, save me! Oh, please!" the woman shouted.

Grace helped William back to his feet. They peered over the rim together. Lady Lira was in the center of the lake now, thrashing to stay afloat. Her skirts were ballooned like a big black lily pad, half-submerged in turquoise waters. Even from a distance, her hooded face looked unutterably forlorn.

Grace felt a twinge of pity. "Can we just let her drown?" she asked. "It seems too awful. Her marmots have changed; maybe she can too."

William delayed an answer. His arm still burned, his head still swam. Charity he could resist.

"How would you get out to the center?" he said.

"We got there before," she replied. "Maybe *we* could get there again."

But even as she spoke, a change came upon the lake. First they noticed a churning of waves—more than Lady Lira could have stirred up herself. Then, one by one, the broken bits of snow disappeared from the water. They simply melted away. Steam began to rise from the surface, surging to the rim, blasting them with warmth. Beads of water condensed on their faces. Their parkas became too hot.

Then the turquoise waters stank. The lake began to roil in earnest, like a noxious soup that was almost ready. Lady Lira tossed in the seething. She was barely visible through the steam. Grace caught one clear glimpse of her face. It was dark and contorted, a very emblem of despair. Her cries for help were finished now. All they could hear was a drawn-out wailing, inarticulate, fading fast.

And even this was not the end. Through the mist—did they not see it?—a mottled head thrust up from the water, bloated beyond all size. It carried with it a murky glow that disillumined the crater. Smoldering eyes, yellow like jaundice, seized on their prey. The great jaws opened. There was one brief glimpse of the oozing cavern, haven of all appetite. Then it too was swallowed in steam.

In a twinkling of an eye the wailing fell silent. All that was left was an empty simmer.

20

EVEN AS GRACE AND William watched, the lake changed again. The steam blew away, the churning subsided, and all was as it had been before. Pale blue waters, cold and clear, lay quietly at their feet. The broken cornice across the crater remained to remind them. That was all.

William checked the gash in his forearm. But the wound was gone. He rubbed the place. Where once there had been a trenched-in slice, there was now not even a scar. Wholeness of flesh—he marveled at it. For the second time that morning William felt he had awakened from a dream.

He turned to Grace, but she was gone. She had drifted from his side to the summit's outer edge and stood surveying the lands below.

She beckoned him. "What are those?" she called, pointing beneath her.

William joined her and looked out. Dark forest spread from the base of the mountain. By now the sight was familiar. But just a few miles distant the forest expanse was mingled and mangled with huge brown clearings. The whole was like a patchwork quilt in which the brown patches outsized the green ones.

"Clear cuts," he told her.

He pondered this. Lady Lira was gone, the marmots freed, the lake restored, his wound healed—but why had the scars on the land returned? Scars? He wondered at his choice of words.

"I think," he said, "we can go home how, Grace."

"Home," she repeated. "There's no place like home."

She thought it over while William retrieved their packs and rope from the northern rim. But when he returned, she was not contemplative—she was enormously hungry. Chambers, they found, had packed away two bottles of soup and a loaf of bread. So they had at it. The soup was tasty, the bread quickly broken. The marmots gathered in a fawning choir and wheedled for every sip and crumb they could possibly get. They got more from Grace than they got from William, but even he was generous with the cup.

When the feast was finished, they roped together and plunge-stepped off the summit. William knew of another way down, longer but gentler, and Grace was relieved. They descended east towards the climbing sun, and descent was sweet. Their feet floated lightly, free as stray bubbles. Their eyes drank in, not columns of steps, but whole world views in terrestrial flavors. It was effortless return, peace with honor, and after a while Grace found herself wishing they never would get to the bottom.

Did the marmots wish the same? On left, on right, they shot down the slope, careening by like playful otters. Some slid on their bellies, sending up spray; others surfed the snow on their backs and waved their paws in air. Whichever way they went, they piped with glee. Whichever way they went, they looked uniformly ludicrous. Grace shouted her laughter to let them know.

When crevasses put a halt to their sliding, the marmots found new sport. In twos and in threes they jumped the rope like dolphins leaping a bowsprit. Grace waited her chance, flipped the line, caught one in midair. "Got you!" she cried. The unlucky marmot spun down on his back. This made good game. But once the marmots were on to her, she couldn't trip a one.

At length the snow gave way to ice, the ice to rubble and rushing waters. Off came the rope, off came the creepers, gladly discarded like chains and shackles. On they descended through braided streams, through dusty moraines, until they came to a meadowland so green, so new after ice and rock that Grace was glad they had got to the bottom after all.

In the middle of the meadows they found a trail, and William said it would lead them close to Chambers's cabin. So they took it. On flat-packed earth their feet found rest—no rocks, no holes, no half-carved steps. They quietly filed through hemlock groves and lupine gardens, sunlight and shade; and every dip in the winding path immersed their feet in a foaming stream. Grace now knew what she had not known—that walking in such a place was good.

Behind came the marmots, a silly parade of them, nibbling by the way and shoving one another into every stream that offered. Yet every time Grace turned her head, there seemed to be one marmot less—although she could not be sure of it since she had never counted them all in the first place. But one chance look confirmed her suspicion. Flashing across a grassy knoll were two silvery marmots, homeward bound.

And so the rest of them departed, singly or in pairs, until one marmot only, the smallest and the plainest, was trotting at her heels. And then he too was gone. She did not hear him leave, but suddenly there came a *peep! peep! peep!* from a rocky outcrop above the trail. She turned and saw him, balanced precariously on his hind legs, waving his paws to keep from falling.

"Good-bye," called Grace. "Good-bye, little marmot." She waved her hand slowly. One, two, three tears ran off her cheeks and fell to the earth.

But she did not have long to be sad. Around a bend in the trail marched Lance himself.

"Hey! hey! hey! hey!" he shouted. Anything but aloof, he clapped William on the shoulder with a healthy swat and gave Grace a hug so unabashed she wondered why this was only the first.

"You're all right!" he exulted. "You look all right, anyway. Me? Sure. Don't worry about me. So what happened? Did you find the ax? Did you give old Lira what she deserved?" He danced on his toes and shadowboxed in air.

"Well," said William, "what she deserved, she may have got." He held out the ax for Lance to see, but Lance hardly gave it a look.

"How was it, Grace? Were you scared?"

"Me!" said Grace. "Of course not."

Then she laughed so long and so hard that she got the hiccups, and every time she hiccuped she laughed again, and everyone with her. They could not help it. Soon all of them collapsed on the grass, holding their sides and pleading with one another to stop; but the slightest word, the least gesture, set them going again. In the end they lay on their backs exhausted, utterly inert.

"Ahh," said William, and he sighed for all.

They remained on their backs and watched the sky and found their breath and felt the turf all cool beneath their shoulders. It was a good place, a quiet place, a place to hear the breeze and touch the sun, to watch lupine bloom and lupine wither, to taste the snow and sniff the rain, and having done all this, to listen to the meadow streams fall down into the forest. It was their place, and not their place, which is why they could stay, and why they had to leave.

At last they sat up, and William asked Lance since when it was he had been so healthy.

"I can't tell you much," said Lance. "This morning I woke

up, that's all. The sun was in my eyes, and there were ants in my shirt. My stomach was wasted. I was lying on the ground inside this old stone foundation that was all sort of overgrown. Sir Chambers wasn't there, and neither was his cabin. I guess I was lying in all that was left of it. So I went down to the lake for a drink, and who do you think I met there?"

"Henry the Eighth," said Grace. "No? Prospero, then. Caliban meets Prospero."

"Oh, come on," he told her. "It was your uncle, Grace. I could tell by his eyes. And his beard too."

"You could tell he was my uncle by his beard?" Grace mocked.

Lance ignored her. "His beard is awesome. I'm gonna grow one exactly like it. Anyway, he just walks up and asks if I want any huckleberries. I go, 'No thanks,' and he laughs like crazy. I thought he would bust.

"Then he tells me who he is, and we walk around the lake, and he points to some smoke on top of the mountain. He's real serious now and sort of choked up. 'Do you know what that is?' he says, and I say, 'No,' and he says, 'The smoke of her burning. It has to be.' I didn't ask him what he meant. He claimed it was a good sign, but you never would've guessed by the way he looked.

"So we go on a little further around the lake, and suddenly he asks me a question. 'Lance,' he says, 'are you afraid of me?' He's sounding pretty stern now. 'I don't think so,' I say. 'Then don't be afraid of Grace,' he says. 'She's been given eyes to see, but she doesn't see anything that isn't really there. She's part-fairy. What you need to know is that's nothing too strange.'

Then he said if he told me about all of *my* own parts, I'd be truly terrified. So I asked him not to. And then he says, 'I will tell you a little. You must fear your own appetite most of all. Much there is that should not be eaten. Satiety brings ruin.'

"When we'd gone about halfway around the lake, he gave me three small biscuits and pointed me over a rise to the trail. He said if I walked this way, I would meet you both. So I did, and here I am, and here you are. And here, I saved two of the biscuits for you."

He held them out. Grace took one shyly, William the other.

"Is Garth still at the lake?" she asked. "Did he say he would wait for us?"

"He didn't say," Lance replied.

As it happened, Garth was waiting. In late afternoon they left the trail and crested a rolling divide. Heathery slopes fell away at their feet to the lake they had known. The cabin was gone, as Lance had said. But standing in the ruins of its foundation was one man alone, easily marked by the whiteness of his hair.

"Uncle Garth!" called Grace. She flung off her pack and broke like a deer across the heather. It was a long way, but the farther she went, the faster she ran and the higher she leapt the boulders and gullies. And then she was there, gasping for truth, crushing herself in her uncle's arms.

"Poor verdant fool," he said, gathering her in. "You cannot outgrow who you really are. You cannot do it."

She buried her face in his full white beard and never thought to reply.

At last, William and Lance approached with much shuffling of feet, and Garth greeted them both. Grace swung around, still clutching his side like a long-lost daughter, and smiled brokenly, sniffling at odd moments. Lance felt his own eyes begin to brim, though he fought it very hard. But William had business to attend to.

"Your ice ax," he said, and held it out to Garth.

"Not mine any longer," Garth replied. "So much as any of us ever possessed it, the ax is now yours, William. And when time is full, you too must pass it on."

"But what shall I do with it?" he asked.

"You might as well ask what it shall do with you," said Garth. "When the time comes, you will know. By now you have learned that much. It is a very old ice ax. Even I know little about it. The shaft was cut from a branch of a tree in the Land of Four Rivers. What sort of tree we do not know, except that it was pleasant to the eye. The metal of the ax seems to be of no one kind: now silver, now iron—for some, in fact, lead. Keep the ax well, William. Use it as you are used by it."

"I will," said William. He looked utterly meek.

Then he remembered something he felt obliged to report. "Her marmot got away," he said. "He wasn't changed like the others. Do you know the one I mean? She called him James."

"I know that one," said Garth. "He is part of her, and he will stay that way even now that his mistress is gone. As long as he is loose, you will have a task at hand.

"But for now," he continued, "come with me, William. It's time at last we returned to the trailhead. If we leave right away, we can reach the Demaris Cabin just at nightfall. There is someone there I would like you to meet."

"What about us?" cut in Grace. She drew away, hurt. "Can't Lance and I come too?"

For an answer he pointed to the eastern horizon. A swerving line of bright orange packs was dropping from the rise. There were five in all. The packs collided, jolted to a stop, and voices floated across the heather upon the evening air.

"Who's got the map? We gotta make sure this lake is the one."

"Hey, it's right in your hand."

"What are we stopping for? Let's just get there."

"Yeah, my feet hurt."

"That's gotta be it."

"Uh-uh, look. The map shows two lakes. This is the wrong one. I'm positive."

"Who cares? Let's go! It's not gonna stay light forever."

"Okay, forget it then. If we get lost, it's not my fault."

"Hah! Nothing's ever your fault."

With that the flaming caterpillar launched itself again. Illogically, circuitously, it found a way to the shore of the lake, and there it made its final collapse.

Please, thought Grace. *Oh, please.* She turned to ask Garth if they really had to. But Garth and William were gone. She saw them striding in the distance over open fields of heather, already small in the westering sun. As if by signal the two men turned and waved. William swung his ax aloft. It glinted in the light. Garth's white beard shone golden now, like the evening snows upon the mountain.

Grace looked at Lance. They both shrugged. Then, very shyly, she slipped her hand in his. Side by side, they stepped out from the ruined stones and slowly took their way to the lake.